# TRIUMPHS AND TRAGEDIES
Twenty-five aspects of the life of a Liverpool Sailor.

# TRIUMPHS AND TRAGEDIES

Twenty-five aspects of the life of a Liverpool Sailor.

## Peter Wright

iUniverse, Inc.
New York   Bloomington

iUniverse books may be ordered through booksellers or by contacting:

iUniverse
1663 Liberty Drive
Bloomington, IN 47403
www.iuniverse.com
1-800-Authors (1-800-288-4677)

Because of the dynamic nature of the Internet, any Web addresses or links
contained in this book may have changed since publication and may no longer be
valid. The views expressed in this work are solely those of the author and do not
necessarily reflect the views of the publisher, and the publisher hereby disclaims
any responsibility for them.

ISBN: 978-1-4401-6814-7 (sc)
ISBN: 978-1-4401-6815-4 (ebook)

Printed in the United States of America

iUniverse rev. date: 10/08/2009

# Foreword

In spite of the rather tattered life I have led, I have managed to resurrect from the ruins some memories I don't want to forget, and have put them in story form. Each story has a special place in my life: nostalgic or poignant; exciting or terrorizing; angry or stimulating, they all fit exactly into the jig-saw of the last eighty-one years I've been around.

You'll find a few essays too. There is a sideways glance at humor in these works; they are descriptive pieces about pivotal times in my life: my alcoholism, my wife's cancer and my own recovery: all redemptive.

I hope you enjoy them

Peter J. Wright

# Part One
## Schoolboy Stories

# Patrimony

## "Forgive things darker than Death of Night"

*When I was ten, my father drowned in the cold grey waters of the North Sea. His death bankrupted the family and left me, the third-born, feebly struggling in an attempt to establish my identity, and some kind of self-value. During the next forty years, I occasionally allowed my spirit to travel eastward to his murky burial place ninety feet beneath the surface. And there I lingered, deliberating death's mute cloak that blocks out all reason, invites recrimination, and often cruelly foils closure. I asked his spirit, not why he had ignored me, but rather, what had I done to deserve his disdain. Ever desirous to please him during the short life span I had known him, so that he might take my hand and hold me close, he had ever turned away from me, and had now abandoned me forever. To whom will I now turn? Who will tell me what I lack? Who will be my man?*

\*

**Bristol, England. April 28 1937.** My mother, usually buoyant and full of chatter, seemed ill at ease when I got home from school. After a silent meal she told me to get my homework done and to get ready to accompany her down to the Bristol City Docks to see my father off to sea. Delighted but curious, for we had never done this before, I was wise enough not to ask her why, fearing she would change her mind. My eight- year old sister Pauline, two years my junior, was left with our landlady.

*Alecto*, a small coastal vessel with a tall, skinny funnel from which dense smoke constantly poured, and of which my father was second engineer, lay quietly alongside the wharf waiting for the tide, her pale lights yellow in the evening mist. From the bell tower of nearby Saint Mary Redcliffe Church, the changes were being rung, a melodious cascade of pealing tones filling the evening air, soothing, inspiring.

I guided my mother's feet as she climbed the gangway, and clutched her hand as we struggled crabwise along the narrow alleyway that led to the engine room entry. My ever-present anxiety was allayed when the ship's cook surprised us at the galley door.

"Oi 'ope you'm don't mind, Ma'm, but Oi got a piece of duff for young Master Peter 'ere. Oi specs 'e's 'ungry." He smiled at me over the top half of the galley door. Turning to my mother he said, "Mr. Wright be still below, M'am, but I specs 'e'll be up shortly."

"Thank you, Mr. Wiggins. You're very kind." My mother looked meaningfully at me. I thanked the cook, and for a moment enjoyed the delights of raisins in sugared dough without the stress I usually experienced when my father was around.

My father's tiny cabin lay at deck level at the after end of the engine room. It contained a six-foot bunk under which six drawers were fitted: an oil cloth covered settee lay across the after bulkhead below an eight-inch porthole, and a water compendium, a simple contraption that incorporated a wash-hand basin, mirror and soap dish, under which was located a bucket to catch the waste water.

My mother told me I could go outside but had to stay on the engine room upper grating. She looked drawn and sad sitting on the settee with one hand clasped in the other. I echoed my thoughts and asked her what was wrong. She simply shook her head and looked away.

With my elbows on the polished steel rail, I peered down into the steamy depths of the engine room, wondering precisely what my father did when the ship was at sea. He was an officer so I expected him to stand-by giving orders and making sure things went right. I had to admit, however, that I'd never seen him in a uniform. As I stood there, I saw shiny bodies climbing about on top of the cylinder heads oiling parts of the pumps, and almost directly below me, a naked man bathed himself from a bucket on the engine room floor plates. All I could see was the broad of his back and the shape of his buttocks. Startled at the lack of privacy and this man's lack of modesty (I would *never* bathe naked in public), I became fixated. A passing greaser noticed me staring down and told the naked man. He looked up . . . *it was my father.*

Fear, shame, guilt, but mostly fear, gripped me as I jerked back hoping he had not seen me. The enormity of my sin, for to see one's parent naked must surely be the most mortal of all mortal sins, cloaked me in a hot blast from hell.

He said nothing to me when he came into his cabin dressed in a clean boiler suit, but fixed me with a glare and merely nodded his head toward the door. I left them alone and took my sin back to the engine room grating where I gazed morosely at the scene of my crime, a wet patch on the steel plates. Should I tell the priest next Saturday? My mother, perhaps? Unthinkable! There was no escape, no reprieve. It, like many other incidents in the barren territory that existed between my father and me, would simply become part of my life's baggage, to be carried around forever.

My mother and I did not wait until the ship sailed, but trudged the weary mile back to our apartment in silence. As we turned on the swing bridge that led away from the dock, I saw my father waving from the engine room entrance. I never saw him again.

Returning from mass the following Sunday, May 2, our journey took us down King Street and past the pub where my mother and father would have the occasional nip. I felt my hand being squeezed as we turned onto the street where we lived.

"Sweet Jesus," I heard my mother gasp, "it's him . . .it's him . . .he's gone." She had seen a group of people gathered outside the house in which we lived. They carried notebooks. Some of them had cameras.

"How long have you been married, Mrs. W?" "How many children do you have?" As my tormented mother feebly fended off the verbal, almost physical, assault with a gloved hand clutching a missal, my distressed sister and I started to cry. I was not quite sure what had happened, but I gathered that my father been killed. Later, I realized that my mother's strange behavior for the past several days indicated that she knew it was coming.

At four-thirty that Sunday morning, *Alecto* had collided with another ship off the coast of Holland. Of the crew of fourteen, four had been saved; ten, including my father, were missing, presumed drowned.

I vividly remember my distraught mother praying to the Virgin Mary and several saints for some kind of relief. I did not pray for anything; I was too numbed by the disappearance of the one person in the family whom I had never known, and whom I would never now know.

*

My earliest memories are those of familial strife and conflict. Not just the occasional spat, but continual barracking and recriminations. My father, the youngest of four, born into servitude on the estate of a wealthy Liverpool ship owner, had been abandoned at the age of ten by his father, a butler in charge of a large staff. His mother, the laundress on the estate, brought him up in an industrial city on the banks of the River Mersey near Liverpool, where he finished his education at a Church of England parochial school. Like many boys of his age brought up in poor but "genteel" families, he became an apprenticed engineer to a shipbuilding company.

He met my mother by chance after his first voyage to sea as a junior engineer. She, fifth in line of a family of thirteen staunch Irish Catholics recently arrived on Merseyside, fell madly in love with him. After a year of pleading, threatening, agreeing, disagreeing and compromising, they were married in the Roman Catholic Church. Among the many regrets my father must have had during his early years, was having converted to the new faith.

I arrived during the eleventh year of their marriage. It didn't take me long to realize that all was not well in the tiny house in which we lived in dignified poverty. My mother's family, ruled by a prideful matriarch married to an alcoholic sea captain, considered us socially inferior because their oldest daughter had married below her station. My father, an English convert, son of a servant and an *engineer*, was treated like a peasant.

I grew up in this acrimonious atmosphere, listening to racial, religious and social slurs, hiding from physical conflict and watching my father get drunk in his attempts to escape. To add to the general misery, my father lost his job during the great post-World War I depression. My mother took a post as nanny to a French family in Paris. My father must have been mortified. Newly pregnant she took me along for company for nine months.

In 1935, when I was nine, my father was offered a job as a junior engineer on a ship sailing out of Bristol, a southern English port. Fortuitously he took the job to escape the outpouring of Irish malevolence from his in-laws. It was less than a year after our family moved south, that he drowned.

In spite of my mother's protection, my father's moods dominated my life. I spent my young years silently pleading with him to take notice of me, to hold my hand, to hug me. He never did. I feared him, but an innate part of me wanted him, needed him.

\*

After his death I was sent to a Dominican boarding school where my mother prayed I would join the priesthood. As an unstable "mother's boy" filled with fear, I fared badly for three years. Unable to withstand the "ragging" (hazing) I developed two nervous complaints, alopecia and shingles, and spent one whole term successfully recovering from the signs – but not the symptoms. Upon my return to school I isolated and built a wall around my space wherein I felt safe.

All I sought in a father figure, I found in one of the teachers at school. He became my hero, my mentor – and he sexually molested me. Added to my inner turmoil, this most awful of sins lay cheek-by-jowl with the certain knowledge that my father also hated me.

In 1943, much to the disappointment of my mother, I became apprenticed to a Liverpool steamship company and spent the next twenty-three years sailing the oceans of the world. Even though I was barely equipped to face the onset of manhood, my days at sea were rewarding. I passed all the examinations for mate and master and eventually became captain of a merchant ship. However, long before I got command, I found alcohol, that sweet, poisonous antidote to all sorrows, which relieved my tortured mind.

I drank for twenty years, and have now been sober for the same length of time. During the dark years, I sired a large family which I, too, virtually abandoned. Eventually my antidote no longer worked for me, and the abysmal world in which I had come to live, became filled with ghastly paranoia.

Finally sober for a number of years, I found that the image of my father had softened. I could still see him starkly staring at me with those forbidding eyes, but my sense of him had changed. I started to write down my thoughts and feelings, and pretty soon my mind took me to places I had previously dared not go.

One afternoon I sat down with a trusted friend and talked of my father's life and his inability to communicate with me. It came to me that my father's life and mine bore an uncanny similarity, and I came to accept him as he was -- a man afflicted.

My father had embraced the Roman Catholic faith in order to win the love of his life, and had accepted the rules. My arrival was a fortuity of transit, an encumbrance in a life already beset with impossible hurdles. He found some solace in alcohol, and all too soon eternal rest at the bottom of the ocean. I reprimand him for not fulfilling his duties to his children, me in particular, just as I reproach myself for the same omission. But I have forgiven him.

In my twilight years I can give thanks to a man who ignored me all his life, I can say with gratitude that in some abstruse way, I have been gifted with a certain humility from his neglect.

Because of my father, I have learned to avoid judging other people before gaining the full knowledge of their circumstances.

The simple words of a great Scottish poet come to mind.

> *"O wad some Pow'r the giftie gie us*
> *To see oursels as others see us.*
> *("To A Louse" - by Robert Burns).*

# The Loss of Alecto

*May 2, 1937. My father dies at Sea*

S.S. *Alecto,* a 1,000 ton coastal steamer, lay starboard-side to-berth **G,** Swansea docks loading tinplate in bundles for Rotterdam, Holland. Loading would be complete in an hour, at about 17:30. The second mate Mr. Ellis, a Swansea man, had attended to the loading so far, and was anxiously waiting for the captain, the first mate, the chief and second engineers to arrive from Bristol. The train had left Temple Meads station on time but had been held up somewhere and was now due in Swansea at 16:30.

At 16:45, the Bristol portion of the crew arrived, much to the relief of Ellis, who could shed the burden of responsibility onto the shoulders of William May, first mate.

"Let me know when you have everything secure for sea, Billy. I'd like to get out of here before this fog sets in," Captain William Austin mentioned to the mate

"Aye, Cap'n. Shouldn't be too long after the last load goes in," he replied. Purchased from Coast Lines Limited eighteen months ago for £5000, *Alecto* became a valuable addition to the new owner's fleet of small coastal traders. Each with a carrying capacity of about twelve hundred tons, this fleet of coasters kept up a regular trade between the Bristol Channel ports and those on the Dutch, Belgian and French/English Channel and North Sea ports. Two hundred feet in length with a three cylinder triple expansion steam engine situated aft, capable of propelling her in smooth water at 7 knots, a single cargo hold was fed by two hatches and six, five ton derricks. When painted up these little steamers looked smart enough, but were always referred to by the larger ocean going ships, as "scruffy little coasters."

Captain William Austin, a Bristolian, had spent his entire life at sea. Now forty-seven, he had sailed deep water as deck boy, A.B. and bosun. A quiet man who seldom drank liquor, the crews under his command liked him. They liked the 1st mate too, they felt safer still with the pair of them on board.

William May, first mate lived in Bristol, not far from Fred Wright, (my father) second engineer in the district of Bedminster. Both May and Ellis, the Swansea man, had wives and two children each, Fred Wright had four; my sister, Pauline aged eight and me, aged ten, lived at home with our mother, while Margaret, a nurse, and Tom, an apprentice at sea, lived by themselves.

Hazy conditions prevailed from Swansea Bay to Lands End allowing two miles visibility with the promise of deteriorating visibility over the next twenty-four hours.

Without sighting a ship or land, but hearing the mournful tones of the foghorns of Pendeen, The Longships Lighthouse and Lizard Point, Captain Austin, a cautious and experienced coastal mariner, saw his ship safely around perhaps one of the deadliest points of land in the world, Lands End. With a weight off his mind Captain Austin set course toward the Dover Strait, unhappily realizing that that visibility was likely to get worse by the time he arrived at the busy cross traffic from Dover to Calais. Oh well, that is twelve hours away, he reflected; time for some shut-eye.

Ships in a hurry to get to port in busy seaways can be downright menacing especially during poor visibility, and even more so while making it through the Dover Strait. Fast ferry boats on the lucrative cross-channel ferry service, appeared to be unaware of any other vessels that were trying to proceed eastward across their path. With their loud Klaxon horns blaring, they streaked across the bow or stern of not only coasting steamers, but also of large freighters inbound or outbound to or from the east coast of Britain. "Damned ferryboats, why the hell don't they reduce speed?" could be heard from the bridge of every ship in the vicinity.

Safely past the Goodwin Sands, Captain Austin, still muttering about "them disrespectful passenger boats," set a course for the Noord Hinder Light Vessel, some forty miles off the entrance to the River

Maas. Visibility had dropped to about three hundred feet. The ocean air all around was filled with the sounds of ships' whistles, some indicating that the vessel was under way but stopped; others were telling the world that they were making way through the water.

"Half ahead, Billy," Captain Austin told his first mate, "and don't let up on that whistle." The echoes of the shrill, bronchial blast had barely died away when the sound of another ship's whistle was heard forward of the beam – the single long blast of a ship under way and making way.

"Slow speed, Billy. Where do you think he's at?"

"Don't rightly know, Cap'n. Close as I can tell, she's a little on the starboard bow." Mr. May pulled on the whistle lanyard for six seconds.

"Stop engines." Captain Austin suddenly felt more anxious. A minute went by, then a single short blast and the appearance of a red sidelight two point forward of *Alecto's* starboard beam and bearing down on them, a large ship.

At the moment of Captain Austin's command, "Hard a'port," *Plavnik*, a Yugoslav passenger ship on her way from Rotterdam to Dubrovnik, struck *Alecto* on the starboard side in way of the foremast, about one hundred feet from the stem (bow). *Plavnik* did not stop but cut *Alecto* clean in half. Mortally wounded, the fore part of *Alecto* dipped under the sea and immediately vanished from sight, taking with it three men asleep in their bunks under the forecastle head.

The impact threw all the men on watch against bulkheads, out of their bunks or into steam pipes or other obstacles in the engine room. Mr. May, with a last despairing look at his old shipmate, Captain Austin, gave a cry and jumped off the wing of the bridge into the North Sea. Both legs were broken when he landed on some flotsam, probably a hatch board or two, but he was picked up an hour later by *Plavnik's* lifeboat.

Mr. White, chief engineer, who was not on watch and was in his bunk at the top of the engine room, stepped on deck and was immediately carried away by the surging water. He too was picked up. An able-bodied seaman and a greaser, Erling Alffin and William Yates, who may have been in the galley, at deck level, getting something to eat before going on watch, also stepped out on deck and were swept away before the after end of the ship plunged to the bottom of the North Sea. They were saved.

Ten men lost their lives. Captain Austin, still stunned at the catastrophic suddenness of a brutal, senseless collision, went down with his ship, a comparatively valueless tiny coastal steamer.

Robert Ellis, second mate, asleep in his bunk, was a young man would never see his wife and children again.

Three firemen in their bunks in the forecastle didn't have a chance.

Mr. Wixon, cook and baker, asleep in his bunk. Less than a week previously he had given me a piece of currant duff just before his ship sailed on this fateful voyage.

Five men in the engine room died horribly. Fred Wright, second engineer, Mr. Charles, Mr. Sealey, Mr. Patnelli and one more fireman, hurled brutally against bulkheads, pipes and small machinery by the impact, were probably headed for the exit ladder when the after end of the ship tilted forward, allowing 5,000 tons of seawater to enter the engine room through the skylight, crushing the would-be escapees to death before they reached the upper grating. The boiler exploded before the ship landed on the seabed, sending up a cloud of sulfurous steam to hover over the hatch boards and other pathetic flotsam that marked *Alecto's* grave.

At 3:43 GMT. May 02, 1937, Ostend Radio received a message from *Plavnik* that she had been in collision with another ship, near the Noord Hunder Light Vessel.

At 4:47 GMT. May 02, 1937, Ostend Radio again reported that Jugoslav steamer *Plavnik* had been in a collision with British steamer *Alecto* in position 51.34.30 North and 02.23.30 East and that the latter had sunk.

During the interval between signals, about one hour, I believe that *Plavnik* determined her own damage before lowering the boats to pick up possible survivors. Had there been no survivors, the master of *Plavnik* probably would not have known what ship he had sunk until *Alecto* became overdue.

A total of thirteen bulletins from Lloyds covered this casualty, including a statement that underwriters acting on behalf of owners of *Alecto* had implemented a warrant for the arrest of *Plavnik*.

The ringing of the Lutine Bell at the Royal Exchange on Monday,

May 3, 1937, an historic way of telling underwriters and other parties interested in this particular maritime adventure of the loss; showed this commercial disaster to be, in broad terms, relatively minor.

*Plavnik* was duly arrested. Temporary repairs were completed in three days, and the vessel was allowed to resume her voyage to Dubrovnik.

For a couple of years I corresponded with Lloyds and Maritime Museums without success trying to find an answer to a few questions.

a. Was there ever a court of enquiry? If so, where could I read the findings?

b. What agreement was reached with owners of *Plavnik* before she was released?

c. Where can I read the statements made by the four survivors, particularly those of Mr. May and Mr. White?

This casualty occurred seventy-one years ago. I am probably the only one who remembers it, or cares about it. The steamship company that owned *Alecto* no longer exists. The casualty is just an iota of twentieth century maritime history that directly affected ten families.

Ten widows were made that morning and perhaps thirty orphans created. In those days there was no insurance for sailors, who were therefore considered valueless. No compensation would be offered or given except by large orphanages who would take the children away and release them when they were eighteen.

> *"What is a woman that you forsake her,*
> *And the hearth fire, and the home-acre,*
> *To go with the old grey widow-maker?*
>
> Rudyard Kipling

My first instinct upon my Dad's loss was one of relief; then guilt, because my mother was in so much grief. It was as though I had betrayed her. The loss of my dad soon became no loss at all. He became a shade that would occasionally, and without invitation, darken what may have been a bright day. And I would visit him at his watery grave, linger a while and wonder why he appeared to dislike me so much.

In later life, my wife treated me with a little hypno-therapy, and the wraith was replaced by a much kinder memory. In much later times, it became clear to me that his death, just as my mothers and sisters, was supposed to happen at that time both of his and my life. There are no accidents except those which my father owns. He may be back trying again to make another life.

# A Gift Remembered

## A Small Boy Makes a Strange Companion

A brisk northwest breeze carries sounds of the Mersey across the Wirral peninsula like passages from the Bible, reminding the living to pray for sailors in peril on the sea, and not forget the widows and orphans of those drowned. The psalm of the foghorns, ships' whistles and the dirge-like clank of the middle-ground buoy, which marks the western end of the Pluckington Bank, were my lullaby. Another poignant impression of that tear-stained face of England ten years after the slaughter was over, was the hush that settled over the crowd at the Cenotaph on Armistice Day, November 11, a few seconds before eleven o'clock. Clutching my mother's hand, I would squeeze tightly when the gun went off. Curiously peering up into her face, I wondered about the tears on her cheeks as the plaintive notes of the Last Post echoed across the cobbles. At that time of my life I knew nothing of my Uncle Tom who had been killed in France in 1918 a few weeks before the end of the war.

A few days later a knock on the front door brought my mother out of the kitchen wiping the flour off her hands, and telling me to stay back while she undid the front door bolt. From the safety of her protective skirt I peered up and saw, framed by the doorway, a tall scarecrow of a man dressed in the tattered remnants of an army uniform. A greatcoat with several buttons missing pinned together at the bottom, barely disguised his mutilated body. An empty sleeve sewn across his chest matched a pant leg which hid the stump of a leg.

Leaning heavily on a crutch, the wind catching the tail of his coat in a sudden gust, he smiled down at us and touched the peak of his cap. His name was Alex McKye, once corporal in the Royal Welsh Regiment.

"Mornin' missus," he wheezed through a bushy, red beard, "Have yis any use for a notion or two t'day?"

Opening the lid of a cardboard attaché case slung around his neck, he displayed a handful of toothbrushes, razor blades and boxes of "Clipper" matches. A row of medals hung suspended from inside the lid.

"Whatever ye can afford, missus," he said, rearranging the contents of his case with a dirty forefinger. "A penny? Tuppence? Just so's I can get a cup o' tea."

The internal struggle lasted but a few seconds before Mama opened the door wider and said,

"Won't ye come on in out of the wind, man, and rest a wee while?" To my horror, Mama let him in.

I watched him close the lid of his box and struggle crabwise through the front door. Once sitting at the kitchen table, he unbuttoned his greatcoat, let out a great sigh and closed his eyes.

While Mama set about preparing him a bowl of porridge, I eyed him cautiously from the far end of the table, my attention focused on his blotched, scarred face which, he told us later, was caused by mustard gas at Vimy Ridge.

Later, no longer frightened of him, I would sit next to him while he told Mama about the terrors of war.

As the weeks went by, Alex appeared regularly at the front door at eleven o'clock each Thursday for his weekly meal and a chat. I noticed that each time he came, he seemed brighter and cleaner. His once-unkempt fingernails were trimmed, as was his red beard, now washed, and noticeably flecked with grey. When a knock on the door announcing his arrival, Mama would go to the mirror and set her hair straight.

I came to trust this mutilated man. I felt warm and at peace sitting next to him. One day after he had left, I asked Mama why he came here all the time. She picked me up and whispered in my ear "Alex McKye is dyin', darlin'. He's bidin' his time just waitin' for God." I tasted her tears when she kissed me.

I knew from the terrible cough that he was very ill. Every so often his body would be wracked convulsively, and he would wipe away a thin trickle of blood from his chin.

"Phosgene gas at the Somme," he told us after he had regained his breath. "I'm one of the lucky ones, laddie. Most of me mates died after taking one whiff of that stuff." After a short pause, he went on, "Lost me arm and me leg at the second Somme – and that was the end of the war for me." Alex gave a little twisted smile. "Aye," he muttered, "I was lucky, 'cos we left 20,000 of our lads on the field, dead and dying."

I heard my mother whisper, *sweet Jesus*.

He held my arm for a minute or two and gave me a bright smile. "All them fellers is not forgotten, y'know, laddie, for every spring when the flowers start to come out, a red poppy grows in the exact place where those soldiers died." I believed him, and part of me wants to go on believing.

I think he fell in love with Mama -- and she with him. I used to watch them talking over that old wooden kitchen table. I heard Mama tell him how her brother, Tom, had been killed by a sniper's bullet three weeks before the end of the war, and saw how Alex put his hand over hers. I did not understand much of what was going on. What was a sniper? What really happened to my Uncle Tom whom I did not know? But I knew that this war they spoke of was a terrible thing. Men were cruelly killing other men for no apparent reason.

In the spring of the following year Alex's visits became less frequent. By May they had stopped. Every day, all summer long and halfway through the autumn, I watched through the front window for his gaunt figure to lurch up the road. My tears dried but my heart continued to ache. He never returned.

This clear memory of Alex is an everlasting poppy in my mind. I reached out to him, and he approved of me – a priceless gift for a small boy.

# A Death at Ėtaples

## *My Uncle is killed in France*

After Alex, our dying mendicant soldier, left that autumn day in 1929, never to return, I started having nightmares of Flanders Field strewn with poppies which opened as I drew near, spilling blood on my feet. Or I found myself lying in the mud with Alex's grinning skull an inch from my face. Mama did her best to comfort me, but I became increasingly afraid to go to sleep. Even with three of us in one double bed, Tom and Pauline on the outside and me in the middle, I lay awake long after they had gone to sleep, fretting, wondering and imagining. I became obsessed with the Great War, unhealthily perhaps, for I would find pictures of a battlefield in which the bodies of dead soldiers lay in grotesque positions, peer at their disfigured faces and wonder what their last thought was, or if their mothers would ever see the picture I was looking at and recognize them. How terrible, I thought, to see the mangled remains of one's son in a glossy magazine.

When Alex and Mama had talked over the kitchen table, she had mentioned my Uncle Tom, killed in action a few months before the armistice. His death haunted me for years. Even today I have not been able to let go of the manner of his dying. In war, all death in battle is impersonal in many ways, especially that of soldiers on the field of battle.

Shortly after my uncle was killed, a young infantry officer named Wilfred Owen died under circumstances similar to hundreds of thousands of other young Englishmen, killed in action; died for his country, slaughtered! Wilfred Owen was a subaltern, but primarily a poet and a humanitarian. His war poems are filled with tragic reflections from the eyes of the soldiers with whom he fought, and his own personal agony. Devoted to his mother, he wrote many hundreds of letters to her from the front line describing his thoughts and emotions and, in vivid detail, his view of war and what it did to his men. He wrote, "But chiefly I thought of the very strange look on all the faces in that camp: an incomprehensible look which a man in England will never see, though wars should be in England; nor can it be seen in any battle. But only in Etaples. It was not despair or terror; it was more terrible than terror, for it was a blindfold look, and without expression, like a dead rabbit. It will never be painted and no actor will ever seize it. And to describe it, I think I must go back and be with them." (Wilfred Owen Killed in action 1918)

When I think of Wilfred Owen, I think of my Uncle Tom Rodgers, buried at Étaples. The two are inseparable. They represent destroyed innocence and the disgrace of all humanity. The following is an account of my uncle's death as I imagined it during my childhood.

Étaples, France. September 21, 1918. Far to the south, over the River Somme and perhaps as far as Soissons, the faint *C-R-U-M-P* of heavy guns rippled the silence at the war-torn farmhouse where a German soldier lay slumped against a perimeter stone wall. Like abstract reminders of Calvary, the few trees left standing pointed stark imploring limbs skyward. No birds sang.

The soldier unbuttoned his tunic and let it hang open allowing a warm summer breeze gently to massage his emaciated, lice-infested frame. His grey, peaked fatigue cap lay beside his rifle. At forty-six, he smiled grimly to himself and thought, I ought not to be here; anywhere but here. He closed his eyes for a few minutes allowing the warmth of the sun to invade his body. For the briefest time, the war ceased to exist. A distant, faint *clink* of metal against metal, acting on his nerves like vinegar on an open wound, jerked his eyes open. He leaned sideways, steadying himself with one arm and peered around the corner of the wall.

Eight hundred meters away and slightly below him the enemy had ceased their pursuit and taken up a position in a shell crater. The noise of their laughter, like insults, drifted up the hill. Pricks, he thought, they had plenty to shout about, they were winning! Does that mean we are *losing?* It didn't make sense. A few months ago, Paris was a gunshot away. French and British troops were on the run. Then the Americans had joined in. Nobody thought they would. He heard that these green troops had halted the German push at the St. Mihiel Salient, taken the position and signaled a general advance along the entire front. He sensed that this time he would not be back. The end was near. The heavy stench of death hung over everything.

"*Zuruchweichen! Zuruchweichen! Funf minuten.*" For the tenth time in so many days the hoarsely whispered command to "fall back" had been passed down the line. Fall back where? he asked himself. Into another shell hole? Behind another stone wall? Why not get out of here and have done with it? He sat up, carefully buttoned up his tunic and reached for his rifle leaning against the wall. Wiping the sight, he set the sliding vernier scale to 800 meters . . . .

Fusiliers of the Royal Welsh Regiment, bivouacked about half a kilometer southeast of La Ferme Hirondelle, knew that a German patrol had taken up a position behind a long stone wall and in the farm's adjacent buildings. They had been chasing them since leaving Bac-du-Sud the evening before.

Some of the latest arrivals at the front took off their shirts and lay in the sun, smoking. Others, the old-timers, quietly lay with backs to each other or against the sides of the shell hole reading old mail from home or bits of newspapers. Familiar with the suddenness of death, their eyes ceaselessly scanned the upper edge of the meadow, knowing that this halt was momentary. "Take and hold the farmhouse," had been their last orders. It had been like that for the past three years. Take a village; give it up. Take a wooded hill then retreat. It'll all be over by Christmas they had said; they said that each year before. Like bloody 'ell!

"Hey, Mick." The rasping voice of Corporal Wilkins in charge of "B" platoon, cut through the murmur of voices. "Make sure Brown and Miller 'as enough ammo for them bloody machine guns o' theirs. We'll be movin' out soon. Got to blast them buggers out of that there farm."

Private Thomas Rodgers, used to being addressed as "Mick" since his induction three years earlier, glanced idly, almost insolently, in the direction of his platoon leader and began to put his boots back on. His last pair of socks, lovingly knitted by some old dear back in Blighty, had outlived their usefulness. Toes and heels gone, he'd tied them together and made a scarf. His boots were not much better. Must remember to scavenge a better pair from some unfortunate sod who didn't need them any longer, he thought. Rather than use newspaper to line his boots (the chemicals had caused sores, which festered and refused to heal), he pulled shapeless boots over mutilated feet. He consoled himself with the thought that they were better than going barefoot.

At a crouching run, rifle slung bandolier-style over his shoulder, he made for the supply wagon, stopping at each of the machine gun nests to find out how much each needed.

"Coupla minutes worth, Mick," they told him. "Just enough to scare the bejesus out of them fuckers up there."

"Good lad, that Mick," said one to the other, as they watched him make his crouching way over toward the quartermaster. "Been with the same corps a coupla years now they tell me. Never sez nuffin' ter nobody, 'e does, jest goes about 'is business. I wonder wot makes 'im tick. I'll bet 'e's got somethin' on 'is mind, I do."

Thomas Donovan Rodgers, private # 46894 of the Welsh Regiment, an uncle of mine whose twenty-seven unhappy years on this earth ended before I could meet him, was born in Derry in 1890, fourth in a family of twelve. He lacked the verve and ambition of Leo and Jack, his two older brothers, and enlisted in January, 1915. Vimy Ridge, the Ardennes and the first Somme offensive were mind-numbing nightmares he had endured with a shroud-like hopelessness. The horrors he had seen, agonies endured through those campaigns were minor compared to the horror he had carried with him for the past twenty-four years. Neither the screech of howitzer shells nor the screams of his mutilated companions could out-clamor the agony within his soul.

Reaching the supply truck, he signed the requisition order and took a minute or two to look around him. These warm, bright days are fake, he thought, there's nothin' out there but sickness and death; life's a bitch!

Crouched there amid ammunition boxes, he allowed his mind to drift to his home in Derry twenty-three years earlier. He heard his mother's voice. "Tom! Tom! For the love of Jesus, what've ye done? YE'VE KILLED YOUR SISTER.! Echoes of his mother's terrible indictment once again washed over him. The vision of his little sister, Anna-May, shrieking, twisting and turning, engulfed in flames as he stood numbly by watching, unable to believe that it was real. How was it possible? All I did was light one of dad's matches, and her dress caught on fire. I'm in trouble again, he thought.

Anna-May had died in hospital that same day. He retreated into the darkest recesses of his mind, where, asleep or awake, a wraith of his sister was his constant companion. Thus did Tom grow up alone and withdrawn. Never given the opportunity mentally to heal, he grew up with a distorted perception of life. After his brothers had gone away to sea, he often teetered on the edge of insanity, becoming morbidly obsessed with death.

He found himself lured, siren-like, toward the death and destruction in Flanders. His voracious appetite for news of offensives, casualties and victories in that continental catastrophe were only partially satisfied by the daily newspaper; he had to go and see for himself.

On January 15, 1916, he left Oxton Road and walked down to the recruiting office on Gorsey Lane and signed his own death warrant.

Three years of futile, wanton destruction had passed since the regiment had disembarked at Calais. Seemingly impervious to the many forms of death which assailed him, Tom stoically endured the lice, rats, obscene mud and the screams of mortally wounded men who fell around him and often asked himself why this new nightmare was allowed to go on. When would it end?

"Eight belts each of armor piercing ought to be enough," the sergeant said, "anyway, that's about all you can carry," he went on, laughing, slapping Tom on the shoulder.

Laboring around the edge of the crater, bent double under his load, Tom shrugged the ammunition onto the ground alongside Brown's machine gun post and turned away to get his second load.

"Hey, Mick, don't forget Miller; 'e'll need about the same," yelled the corporal after the retreating figure. "Real funny bugger, that bloody Mick is. Leads a bloomin' charmed life."

Miller had to wait a little longer for his supply of ammunition.

*"Komsofort, Heinrich! Wir mussen gehen."* There was urgency in
that hoarsely whispered plea to leave his hiding place, that jarred the
senses of the lone soldier leaning against the stone wall.

"What the hell's the rush? Get the hell out of here if you want
to. Tell that fucking sergeant to get out without me. I'm staying." He
settled back against the wall and fiddled with the sight on his Mauser
rifle, and listened to the diminishing rattle of water cans and bayonets
as his comrades left.

Heinrich Schmelling, private in the 24th corps, no longer cared.
His thin face, a six day growth of stubble sprouting from it, creased
into a sour smile as he examined a hand where a gold band, almost
obscured by mud and grime, reminded him of a distant day ten years
ago, when it had clasped Marie's delicate hand. The war had been a
malignant pimple on the Kaiser's soul then. Those were wonderful
days, *Idylliscen tagen!*

Then something went wrong, something he never understood.
Perhaps he'd been blind (his mother said she'd seen it coming for
some time). She's just a whore, Heinrich. Forget her. Move on." But
those eyes, those lips and the warmth of her passion clung to him
like a disease. As a worker at Krupp's steel works in Mannheim, he
was exempt from active service, but in spite of his mother's pleas he
was first in line at the recruitment office early in 1914. His marriage
was six years young when he discovered he was sharing Marie with
someone else.

The rail journey from Mannheim to Mainz, and then to Cologne
down the Rhine Valley went by unnoticed; he saw nothing but the
vision of her face and the look of despair on that day. Now on his way
to the front, he thought perhaps he'd been mistaken, that maybe . . . .
but he knew in his heart of hearts that there was no mistake. Litres
of Moselle wine passed up to the soldiers by cheering crowds at each
station seemed to ease the pain.

At Verdun, where the German High Command had planned an
attack calculated to send the French back to Paris, poison gas was
used. As his corps advanced toward the retreating enemy, evidence of
man's unutterable inhumanity became part of his daily life. Yellowing
corpses, some stripped naked, their grotesque cadavers lying in neat
rows behind the open trenches, gave off the stench of chemically

polluted rotting flesh. And horror of horrors, the rats that lurked within, peering between rib bones. Two years of continuous fighting had not erased the memory.

*"Achtung!"* What was that? The unmistakable metallic grating of bayonettes being fixed, alerted every sense in his body, and replaced the horrors of the past with a chilling terror of the present. A cold cramp gripped his bowels. They were preparing to attack! He could almost feel the ominous threat and concentrated hate. He peered around the corner of the stone wall. Only one man was visible, and he was running, crouched, around the left side of the shell crater.

Convulsively he jerked back, taking in a sharp breath, then lay rigid against the wall breathing shallowly. Somewhere at the back of his mind a band played the old Bavarian marching song

"Ich hat einem kameraden, einem bessern findst du nit." Surprisingly, the realization that he was going to die had a calming effect. His thoughts drifted back to Mannheim, and to Marie.

Body shot or head shot? Feverish now, and fumbling with the shoulder strap of his rifle, he rolled over onto his belly, angled the 800 meter aperture over the foresight and brought it to bear between the helmet and the left hip of the lone, running soldier. Taking a deep breath and muttering softly below his breath, "Armer kerle" (poor sod) he slowly squeezed the trigger.

The nickel plated bullet entered Private Rodgers' left temple and exited below the right ear killing him instantly; his nightmare was over. He his body, pinned to the soft earth by the weight of the ammunition, was discovered an hour later when the farmhouse was occupied.

They took him away and covered his face with a blanket. No tears were shed for this lonely enigmatic lad. Echoing the sniper's eulogy, Corporal Wilkinson wiped his nose with the back of his hand and said, "Poor bugger".

They found the sniper face downward on the cobbles ten feet from the wall. The top of his head was missing. Clutched in his left hand was a photograph of a young woman.

Birkenhead lay baking in the afternoon sun on that last day of summer, 1918, the stillness broken only by the sounds of the river traffic on the Mersey. Margaret Rodgers sat alone in the house on

Oxton Road dozing in the rocking chair, knitting needles and half a sock lying on her lap. A faint breeze billowed the lace curtains over the bay windows. Her husband John would not be home until Monday, the day after tomorrow. Leo and Jim, her two best boys, were at sea, and Tom was in France.

A sudden draft of cool air stirred her into wakefulness and she looked at the ormolu clock on the mantle; it was just after three. An upstairs door slammed shut   CRACK!

"Who's there?" She craned forward trying to peer around the door, suddenly afraid. But nobody was there – not any more.

# Travels with Papa
## *My Grandfather shows me the Ropes*

Perhaps the most damning legacy left by the Tudors and Stuarts and their Hanoverian successors was the cruel treatment of the Irish Catholic in the four northern counties of the Emerald Isle. Forced into penury because of their beliefs, they may well have been marked for extinction. They were denied jobs and relegated to a class of their own. Rebellious, as was always their wont, they constantly butted heads with their Protestant rulers, but were mercilessly put down. While English Protestants established their rule over Ulster, Catholics smoldered. They never forgot the outrage.

As though to add insult to injury, the years 1845-46 brought a pestilence that destroyed Ireland's only form of national revenue and sustenance – the potato. There was no other industry. The country went bankrupt.

Fight or flight? For half of the population, about two and a half million, the question was answered with little hesitation. Jobless and penniless in a country infested with Englishmen – and an entire crop of diseased potatoes, they begged, borrowed or stole money and sought passages to America, Australia or, ironically enough, Great Britain, where they thought they might find the other end of the rainbow. Many landed at the great ports of the industrial northwest: Fleetwood, Liverpool and Birkenhead, where the men found seafaring jobs and the women took in laundry or, if they were lucky, skinned their knuckles on the looms of the Lancashire cotton mills. They eventually carved a niche in society, came to terms with the injustices of their host country and settled in detached Irish-dominated communities.

They brought with them their unshakeable belief in the Roman Catholic faith, a prideful arrogance, and an inherent vice – alcoholism.

My mother, Margaret Rodgers, third born of a large Catholic family, arrived in Fleetwood from Derry with her mother and father in 1903. The family moved to Birkenhead three years later, and in 1915, my mother met, fell in love with and married an English Protestant marine engineer. The immediate reaction was tempestuous. She had broken Catholic Law by marrying someone not of "the faith" - and he was an *engineer,* the lowest form of seafarer according to the arrogant Irish mates and masters.

Family links were sorely strained. Catholics, forbidden by canon law to marry people of another faith, were apt to gang-up on those who disobeyed the Pope; my mother was no exception, her family turned on her. And old sailing ship men, who knew that steamships would soon take over the ocean trade routes, justified their conceit by calling ship's engineers *pig iron polishers* and perhaps explaining to their wives that *oil and water don't mix,* slogans that became dogma and buzzwords for dissent. As a four-year old boy, I was terrified by the verbal and physical violence that occasionally erupted in our front room, especially when my uncles came home on leave. I hid and listened to the drunken exchanges.

I clearly remember the mixed feelings I had when my mother got us ready for our ritual weekly visit to her parents, Papa, a retired sea captain, and Nana who lived on Oxton Road in Birkenhead, about a mile away. Tuesday mornings were filled with fuss and tension. My mother rushed about the house tidying up, stopping every once in a while to dress herself, brush my hair, and get Pauline, my two-years-old sister, ready for the babysitter down the street. From the look on Mother's face and the way she talked to us through pursed lips, I knew she wasn't looking forward to the visit. And were it not for Papa, I would have dug my heels in and refused to go.

My mother dressed me in gray short pants, patched across the bottom with a remnant of one of my dad's old suits. As always she insisted I wear a white shirt with a red and blue tie, objections to which were brushed aside with the explanation that "Gentlemen wear ties; common men don't." My mother, carrying her fifth baby, wore a flowered cotton dress and a huge Leghorn hat of matching material.

With her auburn hair pulled back in a bun, a pair of Donegal blue eyes, and a voice like the gentle ripples on Lough Foyle, I thought she looked beautiful.

But amid the distress and confusion of those early years, I found a spark of warmth in the attention paid me by my grandfather, Captain John Walker Rodgers. I think he liked me because I didn't say much. I reasoned this from a lesson learned from my brother Tom, five years my senior. A constant source of worry to my mother, and prone to answer back, I knew that when he said something to vex her, she would box his ears. I quickly learned to keep my mouth shut. Grandpa also took me on voyages to China, a mystical place I knew existed beyond the smoke stacks and masts of the deepwater ships tied up alongside the Floats.

"Hello, Margaret. Takin' the young'un to see your mam and dad, are ye?" One of our neighbors, Mrs.Lynch, a tall, bony woman with a long pointed nose, waylaid us at the end of the street. A local gossipmonger with a rude way of wagging her finger and getting her face too close to my mother's, she added, "And how's the little'un comin' along then?" eyeing my mother's bulging tummy.

"Och, the baby is due in July, and I'm doing as well as can be expected, all things considered." My mother rolled her eyes heavenward, "Yes, we're on our way to see the old folks. Peter here," she gave my hand a tug, "loves his granddad, don't ye laddie?" Sensing that the Lynch woman, a known busybody, was about to embark on one of her gossipy tirades, my mother hurriedly added, "But we've to hurry along, Marade. Don't want to keep 'em waitin . . . and God bless ye." And we left her standing on the corner bursting with scandal.

Of the numerous childish dawdling's my mother had to contend with, fire engines standing outside the fire house, my protestations that we would all go to hell unless we crossed the street while passing by a Protestant church, or a horse peeing in the street, the most irritating for her was when we passed by the Chinese bakery where raspberry cream slices, (we called them "wet nellies",) were congealing in the display window. Even though I had tasted these delicacies through my brother's indiscretions when he brought them home for half price on his way home from school, it was the sight of pastry, cream and jam squashed against the window that lured me mindlessly to lick the outside of the window.

"For the love of God will ye get yer nose off that window, Peter," my mother hissed at me through clenched teeth, jerking my arm, "I'll not be buying any today."

The upper end of Oxton Road was occupied solely by captains, chief engineers and shipping masters. The marine knick-knacks cluttering the tiny front yards of these retired sailor's homes fascinated me: anchors, lengths of anchor chain, and engine room telegraphs incongruously placed among scrubby privet bushes scalped of all but a few leaves. It was there that my mother stopped to get her breath, to straighten her hat and my tie as we approached Nana and Papa's house.

"Do try to be nice to Nana, dear, y'know she loves ye, and don't scowl so." I knew that Nana didn't love anybody. I also knew that my mother wanted to make a good impression with Nana, and I think she mistook my look of resignation as a scowl.

A large cast-iron door knocker in the shape of a lion's head bolted through a highly lacquered front door announced our arrival. When I pushed the eye-high letter box flap open, I was greeted by a whiff of old cooking, but it also gave me a view of Grandpa shuffling down the corridor toward us, buttoning up his fly.

Giving his favorite daughter a big hug he murmured, "Lovely to see ye, Dolly darlin', and the wee, handsome feller here." Then in a roguish tone of mock rebuke he said, "'Tis ten o'clock, darlin' and there's not a whore in the house washed," and slyly elbowed my mother in the ribs.

"Whisht, with yer dirty talk, Papa. Watch yer language with the little'un around," she scolded. Proceeding toward the parlor, or the "Holy of Holies" as she called it, my mother crossed the threadbare Axminster carpet and kissed her mother on the forehead. I was glad that I didn't have to kiss her as well. Nobody in that family, except my mother, ever hugged me, ever kissed me or, indeed, ever addressed me, apart from Grandpa. While I sat on the edge of a velveteen covered sofa which had seen better days, my mother and Nana began quietly to talk.

I never felt at ease in this house, I often caught myself holding my breath for long periods of time, just gazing around at the depressing furniture. Faded, flowered wallpaper hung with the occasional fusty old prints: "Monarch of the Glen" and the "Ruins of Athens" were two

I remember. By squinting at the wallpaper, I discovered that I could form my own imaginary pictures. I liked doing that.

A great ormolu clock, which chimed every fifteen minutes, sat on the mantelpiece flanked by curios my Grandpa had brought back from Shanghai and islands in the South Pacific: wooden heads and an intricately carved Chinese junk. But overshadowing the scene was the figure of Nana rocking gently back and forth in cane-backed rocking chair. Gaunt, dressed in a black serge dress wrapped around with an off-white shawl, she sat obsessively knitting. I hated the rhythmic *click-click --click-click* of the needles. She spoke without raising her eyes. "Dolly! Tell that boy not to drop crumbs on the sofa," or "Tell that boy not to scuff his heels on the carpet." Even at that tender age, I caught the hostility in her tone. Among the many tragedies which had befallen her, I am sure that her daughter's marriage to an English Protestant had been the worst – and the reason she refused to acknowledge any of her English/Irish grandchildren.

Taking a prearranged hint from my mother, Grandpa pulled a gold pocket watch from his waistcoat pocket and announced that it was "time to take young Peter to the next port o' call." Heaving a black alpaca coat over a tweed suit redolent with the fragrance of pipe tobacco and Bushmills Irish whisky, we left, hand-in-hand for China.

Taking two steps to his one, I hurried along listening to Grandpa talking to himself. All I could hear were fragments of his monologues . . . *get there before eleven, so we have* . . . and . . . *put up with thould Biddy.* He occasionally looked down at me and a smile would appear on a face like weather-beaten mainsail, crowned with a full head of yellow-white hair, and framed between the tusks of a flowing walrus moustache.

Down Oxton Road between serried rows of small brick houses getting shabbier as we approached the dock area, on toward the forest of masts and spars reaching up from ranks of sailing ships laid up in the East and West Floats, where one or two master mariners were kept on by a benevolent ship owner to watch over them.

A policeman at the dock gate nodded respectfully and touched his helmet. Grandpa nodded back. Holding my hand tightly, he steered a course between tiers of barrels and huge coils of rigging wire toward the quay. Leading me up the gangway onto the gleaming white, teakwood decks of the full rigged ship, Olivebank, Grandpa introduced me to Captain Olsen, one of the lucky master mariners.

"Ole, it's been a long time so it has." Grandpa shook Captain Olsen's hand heartily. "What shall I do with this wee feller?"

"Bring him below and tell him a few lies." Olsen chuckled. "But he can stay on deck. No harm will come to him." Side-stepping down the steep ladder between these two ancient mariners into the dining saloon, I found myself in a place that thrilled all of my senses.

Unlike steamships, sailing ships have a seductive smell of their own: salt water, oakum, fish oil and Stockholm tar – an unforgettable fragrance. The elegant mahogany paneled saloon, at once a magical place where the captain and officers dined, reeked with the captivating smell of kerosene and coffee. Polished brass port holes and shiny brass doorknobs displayed the inherent neatness and attention to detail of the professional sailor. People who built ships were very clever, I thought. Fiddles around the table stopped the crockery from sliding off when the ship was at sea. The bulkhead lamps were in brass sconces to stop the smoke from dirtying the wood paneling, and the overhead oil lamp, even now moving ever so slightly, was encased in gimbals to keep it steady when the ship was rolling in a seaway.

Soon tiring of watching these old men pour whisky down their throats and listening to them reminisce about stuff I didn't understand, I climbed the companionway onto the afterdeck. Open mouthed at the number of ropes stretching skywards from belaying pins toward the yards where the sails were hung, I wondered how the sailors knew which ones to pull on or slacken off. There were ropes for every sail and spar, all neatly coiled and secured - a place for everything and everything in its place. Now I understood what Grandpa meant when he described something as *Shipshape and Bristol Fashion*.

All too soon it was time to go home. Grandpa, now showing a gentle western ocean roll, nudged Captain Olsen in a friendly manner and said that he'd be back soon – to fill the other leg up.

On the way up the hill, I noticed a change in Grandpa. His grip on my hand was less firm. He seemed suddenly to have grown older. I sensed that it must be something to do with Nana, whom I hated because she was so mean to my mother – and that awful house. My heart went out to him. It was November 1929.

Papa died at home two months later. My mother took me to the wake held at Oxton Road. She cried all the way there and back. A mute onlooker and stricken with grief, I gazed at that old sailor laid out in full uniform, captain's cap and all his medals on his chest, and listened to his drunken friends and shipmates sing "Wrap me up in a tarpaulin jacket, and say a poor buffer lies low, and four stalwart sailors shall carry me, with steps solemn mournful and slow."

In my small world, the full meaning of Grandpa's death did not immediately affect me. I knew that my voyages to China were over, and that I would never again smell the tobacco and whisky when I crawled on his knee. The full significance came later when I was ten – the year my father was killed. I knew then that Grandpa had approved of me.

Thirteen years later I boarded the training ship *Garibaldi*, a ninety-foot ketch, and sailed across Cardigan Bay, taking my first steps to becoming a master mariner. Memories of my travels with Papa came flooding back. As a young cadet standing in the weather chains of *Garibaldi* in a southwest gale, I had an image of Grandpa, a real sailor, dressed in oilskins and sou'wester, rounding Cape Horn on his way to Foochow for a full cargo of tea. I wanted so much to be like him; and in so many ways, did so. Grandpa created a fantasyland for me. It was filled with tall ships, roaring oceans, hardy sailors and adventure. But he also saw my silent plea for recognition and approval. Grandpa made the effort to do the things grandpas and dads are supposed to do. He took me across the River Mersey in a ferryboat where *everyone* knew him.

"How are ye today, Cap'n?"

"Grand to see ye, Captain Rodgers." And I enjoyed every second of it. I was proud of my grandpa.

*

# Brought to Judgment by the Eye

*A schoolboy comes to terms with corporal punishment*

After an eventful voyage to the eastern coast of the United States and back, I sat despondently in the Marine Superintendent's cheerless waiting room housed in a grimy brick building overlooking the clutter of a shipbuilding yard in Bristol, waiting to explain the causes of a careless piece of seamanship during a simple maneuver in Baltimore some four weeks ago.

I was alone in my prison and was therefore able to pace, and mutter to myself quite freely as I went over the details of the accident. Under extremely windy conditions I had been directed to haul my ship, *Perseus,* one full ship's length down a one-thousand-foot dock, a relatively simple move under good conditions. At the time of the move the wind was blowing force 7 from the northwest. Because of anticipated extenuating circumstances, which included the vagaries of the labor union and the possibility that we would lose a day's work, I decided that we would make the move even though my common sense told me that the wind might be a hazard. Things did not go as planned; a head-rope parted and the wind took charge of the ship causing the rudder to come in contact with a piling, distorting the pintle – and demolishing the piling.

Imagining I had a fair and reasonable argument, I began to calm down. Supposing the Super disagreed with me . . . what would he do? Again the panic. I closed my eyes and almost instantly an image of a young boy dressed in a grey and black school uniform flashed across my mental screen. He stood trembling outside the headmaster's room waiting to explain certain damage to a valuable oil painting. *The boy was me . . . I began to piece that afternoon together . . .*

Bender and I, thirteen year old students at a Catholic boarding school in the depths of the English countryside, decided one warm June afternoon to take our slingshots and go hunting in Rockingham Forest. Slingshots were forbidden at that school; we therefore hid them, carefully wrapped and unidentifiable, in a niche in the old boiler room in the school basement, a place made sinful by the nefarious goings-on of the other one hundred and thirty-eight boys whose mothers' intent was that they take holy orders. Few, in fact, did, but one supposes that at one time the spirit was willing.

Rockingham Forest, once several hundred thousand acres and the refuge for countless herds of fallow deer, had been butchered to provide pit props for the Nottinghamshire coal mines. The present day remaining ten thousand acres of deciduous trees still provided enough cover for fox, small deer, rabbits and weasels, and a myriad of song-birds. This was our hunting ground. Each week we would venture forth hoping to add a hide or the carcass of a jay to the game-tree adorned with Mr. Mussen's trophies. Mr. Mussen was the local Forestry Commission gamekeeper.

After two hours of fruitless stalking we had used up all our good ammunition, small river pebbles, and were reduced to acorns.

"Let's go back, PJ. It's too hot . . . and I want a drink." My nickname was PJ.

"Hey, Bender, you know the rules – we aren't allowed inside until after four."

"Oh, don't worry. It'll be long after four by the time we get there." I had an idea he was way off in his timing, but we set off toward school.

The school lay half a mile before us, a huge Georgian style mansion constructed of limestone slabs hewn from a quarry less than a mile away, and erected about 1750. It was typical of the numerous similar country homes built during the middle of the eighteenth century for the newly made Dukes and Earls who knew how to extract money from the House of Hanover.

The old clock over the stables registered 3:30; we still had half an hour to waste.

"C'mon PJ, nobody will know. Let's see if we can find any grub." My friend Bender was my hero and braver than I.

"What if we get caught?" I timidly suggested, my mind already precipitating toward the painful thought of receiving a whacking for infringing school rules.

"Pooh!" snorted Bender. . . "it'll only be a oner." *ONLY one! I had already received one stroke last term – and it HURT.* I had a great fear of being whacked across the bottom with a half-inch bamboo cane.

The old copper hinges conspired to betray us as we slowly opened the great oak front door just wide enough for us to squeeze sideways into the music room. It was here that chamber concerts were held for the intellectuals once or twice a term; Bender and I were not included in that august group. Beyond the music room lay the Big Hall wherein the true pulse of the school could be felt. From the stone balcony at one end of the hall school colors were majestically tossed down to rugby and cricket players who had played with exemplary skill. It was here that the end-of-term plays were performed and Christmas carols were sung by the combined upper and lower school choirs.

Lit only by daylight diffused through a centered octagonal cupola, the hall was a tacit reminder that this school was dedicated to the teachings of Jesus and His saints, for hanging from the figured limestone walls, where space permitted, were classic oils of various saints. St. Jerome, crossed staff in hand, gazed heavenward, beseeching his Savior to forgive him. (Blimey, I thought, what's he done to forgive? He beat his chest with a stone every day as penance.) St. Sebastian, also looking toward his God with anguished face, his body riddled with arrows. (Must have hurt a lot. I sort of liked him.)

Then there was St. Dominic, austere and definitely unfriendly like the everlasting beatitude. (I had never been keen on him.) The remaining wall space was taken up with floor-to-frieze bookcases filled with tomes on the lives of the saints, and, of course, St. Thomas Aquinas' *Summa Theologica*.

A more recent oil painting of the Venerable Bede now occupied a special place on its own on the short wall to the right of the end arch. Our headmaster had completed his masterpiece a short while ago and hung it for all to see and admire. He had even installed a small lamp above the painting to highlight its finer points. Naturally our headmaster's *pièce de résistance* was viewed by his pupils with mixed impressions, but nearly all agreed that it was a self portrait. The resemblance between the painter and his subject, who died in 735 AD. was quite remarkable.

"What the Dickens are you doing, PJ?" Bender's hoarse whisper startled me and caught me in the act of raising my slingshot, firmly grasped in my left hand, to eye-height, while pinching an acorn in the leather thong between thumb and forefinger.

"What? What's the matter?" I hissed back at him.

*"What are you aiming at?"*

"The lamp! The lamp over the picture." ( Did the idiot think I was aiming at the picture?) From this distance I could hardly miss.

The echoes of that single *p-h-u-t-t* as the missile struck canvas had hardly faded before a sense of the catastrophic engulfed me. St. Jerome, unable as he was to tear his gaze away from the object of his heavenly desire, no doubt prayed for my soul. While Sebastian, perhaps too busy with his own problems, surely must have felt my pain, Dominic merely looked on in horror. The aging Bede, however, placid with his recent disfigurement, cast a reproachful right eye in my direction while the other eye contemplated the limestone slab behind the canvas. As I stood transfixed, an acorn fell from behind the canvas, bounced on the stone parapet and slowly rolled toward me. Bender, mouth agape, croaked, "Oh Crikey!" and fled.

It was now five minutes to four. My own Four Horsemen, Time – Personal Agony – Discovery – Punishment, all bore down at me setting in motion my almost spiritless body. Inch by inch I sidled over toward the Venerable until I looked up and saw the magnitude of my crime. Taking several large books from the shelves marked "The Lives of the Saints," I placed them on the floor and stood on them in order to get a closer look at the damage. Like Thomas, Jesus' favorite disciple, I was obliged to place my finger in the place where Bede's left eye hung limply inward, to convince myself that there really was a hole in the canvas. With trembling fingers I pushed and pulled the optical remnant hoping to align it with the other. Then fearing that it would completely detach, I abandoned my efforts and relinquished my fate to the Almighty.

Half an hour later it was teatime. The entire school lined the four sides of the hall, each wall being occupied by the group of boys who filled up one of the dining tables.

The shuffling, muttering murmur of hungry schoolboys died as the headmaster entered the hall and took his place in the middle.

"Upper middle," his nasal voice droned, and forty or so boys scuffled into the adjacent refectory to stand behind their chairs at the long wooden table. "Lower middle," he intoned a minute later. It was when he turned to face the left-side table students that I noticed the expression on his face change – he'd seen his mutilated painting! Without so much as the flicker of an eyelid, he continued to direct the remaining students to their respective tables.

The prospect of severe punishment had become a reality. Nothing could save me now.

"Sit down." The scrape of chair legs on stone floors followed by the usual outbreak of chatter was silenced immediately by the brassy tones of the hand bell on the main table. The stillness in the refectory was broken by the cold voice of the headmaster. "Will the individual who damaged my painting of the Venerable Bede, please see me in my room immediately after this meal."

Bender avoided my glance. While I sat rigid contemplating my bowl of mushy peas and brown bread, the rest of the school speculated on whom the perpetrator might be – and the punishment that might follow. The general opinion seemed to favor the maximum: six whacks across the bottom, and maybe even expulsion.

Only Bender knew the guilty one, but the idea of not confessing, a fleeting thought, seemed to me to be a far greater crime than that which I had just committed. Perhaps I subconsciously knew that I would, in any event, in the end be caught.

As I slowly trod the stone steps up to the second floor and the headmaster's room, I knew exactly how a spy or a deserter must have felt as he was being led out to the courtyard to be executed by firing squad. The fear I felt was blind and numbing, exactly the same fear I felt during an air raid on my home town of Bristol. Botticelli's *The Birth of Venus*, a vivid pictorial of Venus in all her naked adult glory hanging over the stairway, did nothing to budge my fear.

Following my knock on his door, the invitation to "ENTER" sounded like a sentence in itself.

"YOU?" he said, as though he had construed my inaccurate

blunder as a personal betrayal. He stood for a few seconds gazing down at me with two flint-like eyes, a feature which had earned him the nickname, The Bead. "Of all the boys in this school . . . ." He paused a moment . . . "I presume that you are the culprit?"

"Yes, Father." I had admitted it!

He turned his short, rotund figure about and limped over to the window overlooking the cricket field. Silhouetted against the bright summer afternoon light, tonsure accentuated around his orb-like head, and vestments draped to the floor over his narrow shoulders, he looked a benign enough figure. Rumour had it that the headmaster had lost all his toes to frostbite in Flander in 1916, hence the limp.

At last he turned and faced me. "What am I going to do with you, Wright?" A flicker of hope sputtered in my breast. "I know that you are sorely afraid of being whacked, and even though you richly deserve it, I want you to tell me about the . . . incident. Were you alone?

"Yes, Father."

" Quite sure?" I nodded. "Then please explain what happened."

In broken sentences I explained that I had no designs on his paining, but rather on the lamp. His eyes never left my face.

"Well, Master Wright you have a moral decision to make. I have watched certain individuals in the upper make you the butt of their cruel jokes for the past three years. What do you think they will say if you walk out of my office without a whacking?"

I was surprised to learn that he, the headmaster, had known about the ragging I had received since I arrived at the school. It arose out of my original failure to speak English with their Oxford accent, but rather with my own Liverpool accent. Had I ignored them, they would have left me alone after a while, but because I really objected to their mimicry, they persisted. For some reason they disliked me, and that in itself upset me.

It suddenly dawned on me that the headmaster was right. If I showed myself to be a sissy by avoiding punishment, those boys would surely add that fact to their litany..

"You may be sure, Wright, that if you ask me not to whack you, I shall deal out a much more formidable form of punishment. How would you like spend a week on the Penance Walk? (A three-hundred-foot-long gravel path in front of the school upon which the miscreant was obliged to pace with measured step for as long as was administered.)

Three seconds was sufficient time for me to decide. "Can I have the caning, Father?"

From beneath his long white scapula, the headmaster produced a three-foot-long, half- inch bamboo cane.

"MAY I have a caning . . . you wretched boy. Don't forget your grammar or we shall never know what you mean." A small, satisfied smile crossed his face. "Bend over that chair and grip the seat tightly." In the space of six seconds he delivered six strokes with remarkable accuracy.

Tears of excruciating pain welled up, seeped between my clenched eyelids and ran down my cheeks, but as I walked back down the stone steps my heart was full of joy. Shame and humiliation had conquered fear.

A hero's welcome awaited me. "Drop your pants, Wright. Let's have a look."

"Your bum's better looking than your face."

"We'll take a look in the shower when the rainbow comes out."

*. . . the image from childhood faded and I was back in Bristol awaiting my latest fate.*

The pale, sun-bereft face of a clerk appeared around the edge of the door. "The Super will see you now, sir."

Sighing resignedly, I listened to the dying echoes of the *s-w-i-s-s-h* of the descending cane and went into the adjoining office to receive my just desserts.

# The Molasses Gang

## Out Of the Sweet, Came Forth Punishment

My big brother Tom and I were so unalike, that we might just as well have been from different families. While he feared nothing, except perhaps his mother's ire he got into scrapes at school, fought with other boys and was generally, well, just a boy. I, on the other hand, was a timid lad who never said "boo to a goose." Whenever Tom was restricted to the house for bad behavior, he would get me to play his "acrobatic tricks."

The period I am writing about was around 1930 when Tom was ten and I was four.

I don't think Tom could have been classed as incorrigible; he had boundless energy, was strong, but never thought of the consequences of his actions. I of course, adored him, a source of concern for my mother who wanted us to play, but for me not to get hurt.

We had an old iron-framed mangle in the kitchen, tucked away behind the kitchen door. It only came to light on Monday, wash-day. This mangle weighed a lot. Fitted with six-inch-diameter wooden rollers which could be tightened down for better pressure with a screw-down device on the top frame, it was as big as a modern freezer, and had four iron casters for mobility.

When our mother had finished with it, we would plead that she leave it out for us to play "ships" on. Until the following incident occurred, her answer was always "yes." Tom was always the captain, and I was always the chief engineer.

"Okay, chief, we'll take her to sea," and I would screw down or unscrew the iron wheel on the top frame.

"Hard-a-starboard and slow ahead." I would do some fiddling with something, and Tom put the big mangle wheel to starboard. Sometimes we'd go to China, sometimes to South America, but when we were fed up with the game, we'd come home and dock the old thing.

"Stop engines, chief, and finished-with-engines," whereupon, Tom would give the wheel, connected to the wooden rollers by cogs, a mighty twirl. Unhappily for both of us, I was climbing up to twist the "engine" wheel on top and the fingers of my left hand were on the rollers. I let out a agonized screech as my left index finger went through those hard wooden rollers. Tom had the presence of mind to reverse the wheel just in time for me to pull my hand out and display a squashed, bloody finger to a distraught mother.

"My God, Thomas, you're tryin' to kill yer wee brother," and hauled him off by the ear. Poor Tom, I can't remember if my mother boxed his ears, but the threats were terrible. Grounded for another week; I never blamed him because I knew he never hurt me on purpose. On another occasion, he put me on his shoulders, gave me some instructions, which I am sure I disobeyed, threw me off and I broke my right arm.

Tom spent all his legitimate free hours down on the docks in company with another gang of roughnecks, the Redmond boys. Looking back on our early lives, we both seemed to be waiting for a ship to come along and take us away. Both of us missed our grandfather, Captain John Walker Rodgers, when he died. Our ambition did not die, but our main link to the few square-rigged ships that graced the East and West Floats in Birkenhead, ended when he passed away.

Sometime toward the end of the summer holidays, during the afternoon, Tom came home and asked my mother if he could take his brother (me) down Oxton Road to see the ships. She must have been suspicious but didn't ask any questions. She was not very well at that time of year. Often suffering from the effects of rheumatic fever, she would spend many an afternoon in bed with the curtains closed and the door shut

"Alright, Thomas. Do be careful with yer brother, and don't be getting' into any mischief." Turning to me, she said, "Now young feller, go and wash yer hands, face, neck and knees; can't go out looking like a tramp, can yer?"

I declined to hang onto Tom's hand on the way down Oxton Road which led to the dock floats.

"Where are we going, Tom? Is Uncle Leo's ship in?" My Uncle Leo Rodgers, one of the six seafaring uncles with whom we Wrights kept contact.

"No," said Tom looking away, "We're going to see if the Atholl tanker has left the molasses dock yet."

I had heard of the Atholl tankers and knew they carried Black Strap molasses (the third pressing of boiled sugar cane and the most nutritious.) They loaded this treacly black stuff in the West Indies and discharged it into huge tanks in Birkenhead.

"Are we going to get some, Tom?" I asked not knowing what kind of an answer to hope for – or expect.

"I sure hope so." said Tom, "We have to get in first." "Getting in" meant avoiding the policeman on the dock gates. No big deal for an old pro like Tom and certainly not for me at four-foot-nothing.

At a break in the cyclone fence, we slid in behind some pieces of machinery, and commando-like, dodged from coils of wire to railway trucks until we were at the molasses dock. No ship! Eight, huge cast-iron tanks lay in rows of four; conical in shape with a curved dome, and about thirty fee in height, they looked like space ships to me.

"The closest that's open, is second on the right, Peter. Crouch down and run. When you get there, stay on the right hand side so that the Bobby doesn't see you." Tom said, giving me a push.

When I got to the side of the tank, about fifty yards away, I looked up in awe at the size of this huge steel monster. And the smell . . . *pooh* .The strong, sweet, almost chemical smell of molasses almost made me throw up.

The manhole door was unbolted and open. "Get inside," said Tom a few feet behind me, and gently pushed me toward the gaping hole. There were puddles of hardening molasses all the way to the tank which I was trying to avoid. "You're not playing hop-scotch, Peter, get on with it.

Once inside the tank, where the heat and humidity restricted my breathing and the gloom brought on claustrophobic fears, Tom produced two of my mother's silver spoons. They were not *real* silver, but epns was as good as silver to me.

"Scrape the stuff off the sides, Peter, but don't go down to the metal; if you do you'll die." Tom took time out from his own scraping to issue this ominous threat.

"Why would I die, Tom?" I didn't really believe him but I wanted to know anyway.

" 'Cos you'll get iron oxide off the steel, and oxide'll kill you."

While Tom sucked on a spoonful of caked molasses, I nervously tried to wipe some off with my forefinger. It was hard, like varnish, I was becoming less enchanted with this idea of my big brother.

"No, no," yelled Tom, "You've got to dig it off." Whereupon I started to whimper. I had had enough. My pants and shirt had daubs of molasses all over the front, and my shoes were covered in it. Without any desire to taste and, perhaps, enjoy the black swag that my brother was slurping down, my entire focus was on my mother's reaction when she saw us. How would we get out of this? More important, how would I get out of it?

"Oh, alright," my exasperated brother conceded, "but don't tell Mama where we've been – I mean don't tell her we crawled inside a tank; she'll kill me."

As I struggled to get my leg over the bottom flange of the manhole opening, the shoe on my left foot stuck in the sludge at the bottom of the tank, and came off. Tom saw my plight, pulled it out and gave it to me. "Better put it on." He said.

"But it's full of treacle," I moaned.

"Never mind," Tom said, "Put the damned thing on." Tom, too, was beginning to think nervously about the consequences.

"Don't be mad at me, Tom. It's not my fault." There was no answer. I peered up at his face knowing that he was in a lot of trouble unless we could somehow avoid our mother. Maybe she was still feeling poorly.

People on the street were turning to give us a second look. They grinned as they passed. Tom's lips and cheeks were curry-colored and he had brown smudges on his neck and all the way up his arms. His shirt and long pants were smeared with what appeared to be grease, but was in reality, congealed molasses. My condition was about the same except that I had short pants on and my left shoe squished at every step.

My mother was still in bed when we got home, but she was awake. I could hear her coughing. While Tom took the only bathroom we had, I occupied myself at the kitchen sink. While I scrubbed with Rinso and a scrubbing brush, I heard my mother talking to Tom through the bathroom door.

"What are you doing in there, Thomas?"

"I . . . er . . . we got a bit dirty on the walk and we're just cleaning up a bit."

"Cleaning yerselves up?" Her question registered surprised, anxious disbelief. "And where is your wee brother?" Tom never got a chance to answer.

"Och, I *know* where he is." She swiftly came downstairs in her stockinged feet.

"What in God's name are ye up to, young man?" She stood in the kitchen doorway, her arms akimbo, her head to one side and her piercing blue eyes focused on my naked body.

My clothes were in a heap on the flagstones. I was standing on a cane-backed kitchen chair facing the sink. With quick short steps she was next to me in a second. I thought I was in for a lambasting. She picked up my left shoe between forefinger and thumb and dropped it immediately and tasted her finger.

"Ye pair of fiends! Ye pair of black fiends," she wailed, and kicked the pile of soiled clothes I'd discarded over the kitchen floor. I knew that when she started calling is names, she was really upset." I canna get that stuff out, ye ken?" She was breathing heavily." It'll be new pants for you, me boy, and I dinna have the money for it."

In a moment of four-year-old, fear-driven compassion, I got off the chair and hugged my mother's waist. I felt her hand stroke my head – and knew my immediate danger was over.

I think, at that moment, my mother realized that no amount of punishment she might administer to either of us would ever stop us from performing "fiendish" pranks. But, apart from a severe scolding, she took no other action – or did she?

After a weekend of extra house work on our part, always a part-punishment for infractions, and an extra load of washing which my mother did on its own, Tom and I were ready for another school week.

On Sunday evening at 7:p.m, when we all went to bed, Mother called us into her bed room where she did all her sewing, and showed us our "new" school clothes, all laid out on the bed.

"Here ye are lads" She held up the pants that Tom had worn at the

Atholl dock. They looked a bit like a patchwork quilt. Pieces had been cut out and been replaced with similar cloth but of a slightly different color. My short pants had also received my mother's artistic efforts. Our shirts, however had suffered a different cleansing process. Where the molasses stains had been, there was now an almost colorless swatch of cloth –she had scrubbed the spots with Lysol and bleach. My left shoe had been soaped and par-boiled. The treacle had vanished but the shoe was gray rather than black. "If you like, Peter me-boy," she said waggishly (so unlike my mother) you may put black boot polish on it. It's up to ye."

Completely floored by this "selfless" economic move, I made a few feeble protestations, but I knew she had me beat. She knew how particular I was about my clothes, especially those I wore to school or out shopping. We had had screaming fits before about the visibility of darns in the heel of my socks, and other, neater patches in my pants which did not meet my critical standards. I sulked, but wore these awful looking clothes.

I don't think Tom cared too much. Vanity was not in his makeup as it was in mine.

*

My mother never fully recovered her health, and died from renal complications on Good Friday, 1964. I have nothing but fond memories of both.

Following a mass exodus of younger people, Tom and his wife and two kids left Britain and went to New Zealand in 1954. Already holding his master's certificate, he found a job with the Union Company, and sailed across the Tasman Sea between Wellington and Sydney for the next twenty-nine years as mate and master. He died on Christmas Eve, 1982, one year before he was due to retire.

# The Old Belgian Organ
## Caught Running Out Of Wind

Among the sundry lay jobs I avoided at school, were those connected with the liturgical side of the ritual; sacristan, acolyte, altar boy or server--anything that brought me into public focus. I was always an acutely self-conscious lad and imagined that everyone was criticizing me; judging me.

When I was in the fourth form, about fourteen years of age, the head sacristan appointed me thurifer for the upcoming high mass on Palm Sunday. The thurifer is the guy who carries the thurible, the brass sensor hung on chains which contains burning incense. Some of you reading this can imagine how I felt, especially when Sunday morning dawned – horrible. I knew I was going to make a mess of it. If I'd known exactly how I would have made a mess of it, I would have caught the next train back home.

From the sacristy I could hear the organist playing one of Bach's cantata's in the chapel and the muffled coughing and shuffling of a hundred boys getting ready for the weekly injection of energizing Gregorian chant.

"Put the cassock on first, Wright, the surplice over that, okay?" I dutifully obeyed, and in smoothing out the outer garment, the surplice, I noticed that my shoes were muddy and scuffed: too late to do anything about that now.

I had had a few lessons in mastering the art of manipulating the thurible and was, perhaps, less fearful of taking it off the hook in the sacristy than I might otherwise have been, but I doubt that anyone noticed or cared.

46

"No, no. Stick your thumb in this ring – you *are* right handed, aren't you? Okay, then put your middle two fingers in these two holes, like this." The sacristan nimbly demonstrated. I followed his instructions as best I could, but when I was standing at my full five foot nine inches, I had to hold this sacred instrument almost at eye-level so that the bottom container, where all the hot incense was, would not touch the flagstones in the chapel. I might mention here that the thurifer, followed by four acolytes, the deacon and the sub-deacon, then the priest, led the parade out of the sacristy.

Treading ever-so-carefully, almost on tip-toe, I led the procession into the chapel. I was amazed how much noise boys make when they simply stand up; snuffling, sneezing farting and generally being clumsy. Everything went well, even when I handed the thurible to the priest so that he could bless the missal and whatever other objects had to be blessed. When he handed it back, however, I got my two middle fingers where they were supposed to be, but somehow only got the thumb-ring halfway over my thumb. The result was inevitable. With my full attention on manipulating the thumb-ring farther onto my thumb, I allowed the device to wobble, and while I frantically lifted and swung it, the beveled bottom of the incense cup struck the edge of one of the flagstones ejecting hot coals onto the altar carpet, and onto the white habits of some of the monks kneeling at the altars' side.

There was a little pandemonium. While the monks put their own fires out, I tried to scrape the embers back into the brass container. Without even thinking, I picked up a piece of hot incense. Burning and hot, It stuck to my finger of course, and I said "Jesus."

"Don't apologize to Him, Wright, get on with mass." One of the monks with a sense of slapstick, helped me stay fairly calm. The damage was slight, and little was said by the clergy. A couple of them smiled and one or two raised their eyes. For the rest of the school, however, it was a hilarious topic. "Couldn't have seen a better show at Blackpool," one Lancashire lad remarked.

The following week was Passiontide, a week of prayer, retreats, and from Thursday onward, almost continuous church services. Mass every day, the rosary at noon and during the evening, *Tenebrae,* an impressive evening service during which all the candles carried by the congregation (the students), were one-by-one extinguished until the chapel was in complete darkness.

Since we were not a state institution, but governed by the Catholic Church, the good monks enjoined both our parents, and us, to stay at school over the Easter weekend so that we could celebrate Christ's resurrection. Our parents agreed – we had no option.

High mass, as always, is celebrated on Easter Sunday with all the pomp and ceremony the Catholic Church so enjoys. The acolytes and the thurifer had fortunately already been chosen. My friend Bender and I, however, did not escape; we were designated as organ pumpers – supplying air for the bellows of an old Belgian organ, which I believe came over from Flanders during the eighteenth century. "A thing of beauty and a joy forever" (John Keats) might describe this monument to the mellifluous tones that filled our chapel. Ancient though it was, the pipes which extended to the roof of the chapel, had been exquisitely fabricated so that proportions of air into the reeds matched exactly the length and diameter of the vertical pipes. I am very glad that John Keats did not have the opportunity to write about the bellow's attendants on this particular Easter Sunday.

On the plain wooden back of the organ was a spring-loaded three-foot-long wooden lever (pump handle) placed about four feet above the floor and parallel to the back of the organ. At eye-level was a bellows-capacity gauge – a small hole into which ran a piece of waxed twine. The outside end of the twine, wrapped around a bullet-like piece of lead, extended to within two feet of the floor. Inside the organ the twine was attached to a device that measured the input and the expulsion of air from the bellows.

Two inches below the hole, a horizontal groove had been cut and highlighted in red. A typed notice directed the pumper, "Do not allow lead bob above this mark."

Dressed, as always, in our gray pants, white shirts and black blazers with the school tie, Bender and I looked, just as the other hundred-odd boys, like "angels."

When the organist gave us the signal, we pumped air into the bellows allowing him to play another of Bach's *cantata's*. Boring! Bender leaned over and said." Here, you pump, Peejay. I bet I can get that lead bullet closer to the hole without pumping, than you can."

Well, anything Bender can do, I can do better!

It turned out to be quite a scary and intense game. We'd fill the bellows and then watch the lead bob crawl up the back of the organ until fear made us pump madly again.

"Better'n yours, Bender" I would say triumphantly.

"Naw," said he, "just watch this."

Wrapped up in our "chicken" game, neither of us had paid the slightest attention to the progress of the mass. Unhappily for us the *Gloria In Excelsis Deo,* which had not been sung or played since the end of Lent, was a minute away – and we were still playing our silly game.

The lead bob was five inches from the hole, when we heard the fateful sounds of all the stops being pulled out, bass, alto, and treble. With the inrush of air into the bellows, the bob began to move twice as fast.

"Oh, crikey! Pump! For God's sake pump," Bender hoarsely whispered. We both grabbed the handle together. The bob crossed the safety mark.

The opening crescendo of joyous, victorious notes from all ten pipes began as expected, but two seconds later subsided into a piteous moan, like that of a dying steer. Those pigskin bellows became a vacuum. The organist had the presence of mind to push all stops in again.

Sweating, eyes bulging and pumping, our arms flailing like the Oxford-eight on the Thames, we managed to catch the bob before it disappeared inside the organ. Still pumping, we heard the stops being pulled again, and pumped even harder. Now replenished, the bellows fulfilled its obligation to its designer. The school choir now joined in with the motet after the opening bars.

We stopped playing "chicken," and spent the rest of mass figuring out excuses.

*"The handle came off and we couldn't get it back in time."*

*"Bender got an awful cramp in his arm. I didn't have the strength to fill the bellows."*

Blaming the instrument or our own infirmities were the only two avenues of escape we could think of to us at that time. It turned out, however, that we were not obliged to use either of them.

At the end of mass, we were observed by the entire school as they filed out of the rear of the chapel, to be doing our job while the organist continued to play bits of J.S.Bach until the chapel had been vacated. We had the usual joshing from those boys who knew us, but it seemed, for the moment at least, that our pneumatic *faux-pas* had not been heard as anything but a mechanical glitch – except, of course, by the organist. Stephen Barry.

Poor Stephen, a really nice, gentle sixth former, stalked around the corner of the organ, his face beet-red, and confronted us.

"You've ruined my Easter Sunday," he hissed at us scathingly. "Have you any idea how embarrassed you have made me?"

Bender and I looked at each other sheepishly.

"Look, Stephen," I said placatingly, "I don't think anyone noticed the interruption .". . "Of course they did, you nincompoop, of course they did," and he turned and strutted away.

I did see Stephen Barry again, on the stage of the Royal Albert Hall in London, playing one of Beethoven's piano concertos with the London Philharmonic Orchestra.

I also saw Bender again -- the following term

*

# The Collyweston Lunatic
## And Other Scholastic Imbeciles

*"Full of sound and Fury and worth not a whit"*

*Shakespeare*

When I was ten years of age, my mother sent me to a boarding school in the middle of rural England. The school sat joylessly, like an enormous limestone cube, in the middle of a large estate filled with ancient beech trees, toweringly gaunt in the winter and voluptuously endowed with fragrant floral candles in the summer. One of these beech trees I well remember. Perhaps two hundred years old, it had one long branch which stuck farther out from the lower part of the trunk at an angle of forty-five degrees, like the bowsprit of a sailing ship. Of all other beech trees on the estate, this particular tree was known as *THE BEECH TREE*.

Like many other aspects of that school, activities connected with this tree, which I shall explain later, gave me cause to wonder why my mother had sent me there. Known throughout England as a school of "academic learning," and, surreptitiously as a place to study if one were interested in the priesthood, I frequently wondered how so many of the students, whom I considered nothing but hooligans, managed to stay there.

As a young student I ravenously lapped up English history. I became fascinated with the skullduggery that went on when evil forces executed Charles I and abolished parliament, declaring that England was no longer a monarchy but a commonwealth. For eleven years,

England lay in a chaotic backwater. During my study of the decline of order in the late middle ages, it occurred to me that the behavior of the two opposing factions in England, the Royalists and the Roundheads, closely resembled that of our own upper and lower schools, a handful of whom appeared to have few morals and no discipline.

In 1980 I returned to the old school in an attempt to recapture the ambiance, and see where my emotions took me. Abandoned as a school in 1965 or so, the school had moved to Wales. My limestone cube was now a retirement home for the Polish clergy, one of whom was kind enough to allow me to wander through all the public rooms, even to the cellar where many of the steel framed school desks were still in storage.

The magnificent, embossed antique wallpaper that covered the sixteen-foot high walls of the Big Indian and Little Indian dormitories had been removed, and the walls painted. Off white. The manner in which the wall covering had been removed rather than the reason for its removal surprised me. Local workmen had randomly ripped it off in irregular sheets and abandoned it. I remember seeing it for the first time when I was a ten-year-old new boy, and being fascinated by its eroticism. The scenes depicted a tiger hunt, but the East Indian men and women were scantily dressed. There was, at least to my young senses, an air of wanton impurity. I am still curious why those Polish nuns and priests felt impelled to remove that beautiful artwork. It crossed my mind at the time that perhaps the nuns had no breasts beneath those gowns.

The cricket field, once an acre of superbly tended emerald lawn, epitome of a public school's Saturday relaxation, now sprouted wild grasses. However, If I listened carefullyin the still air, I could hear the c-r-a-c-k of ball on willow bat, followed by the desultory clapping of a few bored spectators

The front of the huge house looked as forbidding as it ever had. The enormous copper-clad doors reminded me of beginning and end-of-term days when suitcases were being lugged in or out of the great hall accompanied by the shrill screams of the lower schoolboys. It also brought sharply to mind an oil portrait of The Venerable Bede, an acorn and a whacking.

I looked north toward the Long Meadow, where THE BEECH

TREE, like Tyburn's Gate, came into view. Now almost three hundred years old, the branches had grown bigger, and the bowsprit branch, perhaps a little longer, remained jutting upward and outward symbolizing, for me, the lunacy of some small boys. The tree, apart from being part of nature's magnificent adornment, had also been used as an instrument of torture. At the beginning of term, a few of the members of the upper school would scan the harvest of frightened faces of the new boys and select three or four as experimental specimens. I can hear them now.

"C'mon D'Arcy, don't be a funk. There's nothing to it. All you have to do is relax, and go with the tree. No-o-o-o, it won't hurt!"

The unsuspecting lad would then be led under the long branch, a woolen school scarf wrapped once around his neck, then the rest of it around his body and the bare end tied to the limb. Five or six boys who had pulled the branch down to within four feet of the ground, would then let go. Amid whoops of glee the unfortunate victim became airborne, whirled a couple of times and fell several feet away. I wondered if this kind of behavior typified normal boarding school exuberance. Had I arrived at a school of idiots?

Another incident which raised doubts as to the sanity of some of the older boys occurred after a particularly ghoulish end–of–term play called *The Mummy's Revenge*. The lout that played the mummy went straight from the stage into the junior school dormitory where ten boys, all about ten years of age, were sleeping. The headmaster had deemed the content of the play unfit for those that young. Making gurgling/ moaning noises, he leaned over one slumbering lad and woke him up. The shriek this boy emitted could have been heard in the village. It took well over an hour for the Matron, a homely lady, to calm him. He was sent home two days early and did not return the following term

Had that group of boys who happened to be at school during the war years like me, belonged to a singularly empty headed strain? Had the bombings done this to them? I had been through the Bristol bombings and I was pretty normal – I thought; reserved and painfully shy, but not mad. It worried me that these six or seven boys, whom I considered a threat because they were "raggers" (hazers), were at large in the school. I watched them carefully – almost obsessively. They appeared to have no regard for discipline, or the meaning of obedience.

In retrospect, however, I wonder about my early judgement. Wasn't I crazy, too?

Compared with some of the other Public Schools surrounding ours, we were what might be described as *liberal*. The discipline was severe enough, despite the inadequacies I considered to exist among a certain group of students, but individual free time was among one of the schools' attractions.

Ever since the school had been established in England in 1924, a full day off from schooling was granted every month; they were called Month Days, usually decided upon because of some ecclesiastical occasion, a Saint's day or a liturgical feast. The rules for this day were numerous, but simple – no public transport, no hitchhiking, no casual conversation with strangers, no entering public houses and the usual laws of the land. In addition to the shilling allowed us every Sunday for postage stamps, each pupil could take one additional shilling from his pocket money account. We were allowed out of the school's parameters from 7.am until 7.pm. One of the most common walks was to Stamford, the capital city of Rutland County, nine miles north on the A.43, upon which highway the school lay. Another less popular destination was Fotheringhay Castle where Lady Queen of Scots was beheaded. The ruins of this castle lay fifteen miles away. Thirty miles in one day was a fairly hefty hike. Many lads preferred to visit some of the local picturesque villages, Duddington, Bulwick or Kings Lynn, which one year later would become overrun with American airmen.

In spite of the spooky tales I had heard about Collyweston, one of the villages on the way to Stamford, and the "dangerous" lunatic who lived there, my friend and I decided that another visit to the city made famous by Henry VIII in 1557 would not be too boring. In any case I'd been through Collyweston several times before and seen nothing scary there.

On what promised to be a cloudy/clear day, my friend, Peter Bender, and I set off at 8am. By 9:45 we were outside the Post Office cum grocery store in Collyweston. Not a soul stirred in that hamlet. Excluding the Post Office, there were seven other houses. In one of them lived the dreaded lunatic, the antics of whom had scared some second formers at some time. The stories had been handed down term-by-term getting more grotesque as time went by.

"Y'know, Peejay, I think it's a full moon tonight." The significance of the announcement struck me immediately. Not being a courageous creature, that tid-bit of astronomical ephemeris did nothing but ruin the next five hours of my life.

"Are you sure, Bender?" I watched him carefully.

"Yeah, I'm sure. I looked it up before we left" He was looking away, but I saw his ear twitch and knew that every time he grinned, his ears twitched.

"You liar!" I yelled at him. But maybe he was right after all. I continued my thoughts of the return trip to school in about five hours from now with a certain amount of dread.

The ancient city of Stamford had not changed since I'd been there last. The next few hours were spent looking in shop windows, browsing around antique stores, where the owner scrutinized every move we made, and followed us around instructing us not to touch anything. Mrs. Annie Pruett's Bake Shop, our favorite eatery, tucked in behind St.Martin's Church, was where we spent most of our time. We did justice to a large pot of tea and six currant scones baked and set out royally by an amiable Annie Pruett for a mere sixpence

After an exhausting schoolboy's day, climbing on things, ducking under things, chasing the ducks and walking on grass posted *"Do not walk on the Grass,"* it was time to go. I had sixpence left out of my shilling. I already had it earmarked to spend on a *Gateau Rhumba* (a delicious sponge cake filled with strawberry jam and covered with icing) at our own local village bakery the following Sunday.

As we approached Collyweston our walking slowed to a dawdle. We instinctively stayed closer together. A subconscious dread quite suddenly developed into a very conscious fear. Would we see the lunatic so often spoken of at school? What might be the worst thing that could happen? *"Two schoolboys found bludgeoned to death outside the City of Stamford."* I shivered at the image. Bender seemed so far to be unaffected; he strolled along swiping the heads off dandelions with a willow stick. I knew he was faking.

"D'you think we'll see him?" I asked.

"Who?" He said without looking up.

"Who? You nit-wit, who d'you think? – the lunatic." I yelled.

My attention had drifted from the highway for a moment or two. When I looked ahead again –*THERE HE WAS*, standing at the edge of the road staring at us out of two small eyes that seemed to have little expression in them. He was smiling, or so it seemed to me. Bender and I had stopped not knowing whether to ignore his presence or say, Hello.

We edged toward him with the aim of sidling by and continuing on our way to school. The closer we got the less menacing he appeared to be. Dressed in a country smock, no socks or shoes and an oversized flannel cap squarely on his head, he looked like an actor in a Shakespearean play. Then it dawned on me; he wasn't a lunatic, he was Mongoloid. He had some sort of genetic defect. Back home in Bristol I knew two families with children thus affected; they were a little strange to deal with, somewhat exuberant, but otherwise friendly.

Having recognized his condition I turned and approached him. "Hello," I said, "my name's Peter. What's your's?"

He gazed blankly at me for a second or two, then let out a howl of distress and bolted into the nearest house.

"Now see what you've done mister-know-all? Why didn't you leave him alone?" Bender shouted at me and started to walk away at a fast pace.

Startled by the reaction of my new contact and angry at Bender for being so unsupportive, I thought I would make some amends and started toward the house. I didn't get very far. Standing outside the front door was a man with a shotgun cradled in his arms.

"You'm boys be from that there fancy school down along, I specs. Well, you'd better stay out 'o this 'ere town or you'll be getting' a taste of this 'ere single barrel." Hatless, a great mop of hair sprouting out at all angles and wearing a poacher's jacket, he glowered at me purposefully. I could see his trigger finger twitching. "Ain't you got no better sense than to frighten a pore mazed girl with no sense in 'er 'ead?"

"Excuse me sir," I blurted out, "I was trying to make friends with him – her. I didn't do anything to frighten her; just held out my hand." I looked down the road where Bender stood scratching his stubbly head, his mouth twisted in a grimace.

"Is that'n the boy what made my Mary cry?" The man half pointed his gun in Benders' direction. Without waiting for an answer, he lifted his gun and yelled, "Gerroff with ye, young bugger, afore I lets ye 'ave a taste 'o this'n." He shook his gun menacingly. I didn't know Bender could run that fast. In less time than it took me to apologize to the man and start walking, he'd covered a hundred yards.

I finally caught up with my school friend a couple of miles from school, who by his attitude, wanted to kill me.

"Did you sick that farmer on me, you rotter? I might have known it. Never trust anyone from Bristol!"

"You're just a measly funk, Bender." And that's when we started to fight. Lots of name calling and lots of growling, but no serious punches landed. School blazers and ties suffered. We walked back to school in silence, ten yards apart occasionally throwing stones at each other. The anger dissipated quickly and before we went to bed that night we had made friends. There was nothing, we decided, important enough to spoil our comradeship.

My great friend Peter Bender and I had remained close for six years. We left school on the same day in July 1943: I with great ideas of joining the Merchant Navy and seeing action in the North Atlantic, he with no other ambition than to join the army like his father. He lived in Norwich, a relatively short distance from the school. I lived in Bristol, five hours away by train. On the station platform we strolled to the far end, smoked a Luck Strike cigarette which he had scrounged from some American airman at King Lynn, and solemnly shook hands vowing to keep in touch – no matter what. We never did.

Peter joined the 47th Royal Marine Commando and was killed on June 6, 1944 at Arromanches on that part of the Normandy beach renamed Sword Beach. I learned of his death a year later.

I went to sea.

I am now in my eighty-third years. I survived the bombings and the Battle of the Atlantic, and came out of that conflict unscathed. But many of those "lunatics" I studied with, did not. Michael Gribbin, shot down over the Ploesti oil tanks. Richard Dutton, lost at sea in the Mediterranean in submarines. Ralph Haggberg, shot down over Belgium flying a Mosquito. Ralph Bellamy, killed in action in Germany, Royal Tank Regiment.

The list goes on, but my memory grows dim.

# Part Two
## Sea Stories

# Bristol at War
## *Reminiscences of the Blitzes 1940-1944*

My mother, well equipped with inherent frugality, her Irish charm and good looks, and her eternal friend and comforter, Jesus' mother, entered WWII like a gladiator. If there was anybody in Bristol who could spin the food out, it was she. She was also a natural seductress. I found a distant place to hide in the butcher's shop when we went together to get the week's meat ration.

"Ye know, Timothy – ye don't mind if I call ye Tim, do ye? – I've a household of hungry kids up the hill. I've a lovely ould dog too. He's a Labrador and such a sweet feller. D'ye think ye could find an ould bone with a little bit extra on it, ye understand?" She never failed to bring home an ounce or two extra. I can't remember what the ration per person was throughout the war; it seldom changed, but we kids were never hungry. I believe we were allowed two eggs per person per week, six ounces of meat, four ounces of sugar, one 2 pound loaf of bread, four ounces of butter, and so on. All the allowed quantities were calculated in accordance with a little over the minimum to maintain a normal healthy human being. Exceptions were made for those on special diets and those with special needs. My brother Tom, away at sea in the Merchant Navy, occasionally brought us delights from America and Australia, such as chocolates, nylons and chewing gum. He once brought home several large cans of Australian butter which, upon opening, were found to be rancid. My mother immediately emptied the contents into a large saucepan, added salt and water and boiled the contents for an hour. The result was wonderful, sweet butter. Not one single edible item was thrown away. What we didn't eat went into pig bins, usually attached to lamp posts in the street which were collected twice a week and fed to the hogs.

In spite of the fiercest opposition by the French, Belgian and Dutch forces, and our own Expeditionary Force, the Germans swept across the Low Countries with embarrassing ease. Our own defiant, patriotic songs began to mock us as we fell back toward the Channel.

> *We're going to hang out the washing on the Siegfried Line*
> *Have you any dirty washing Mother dear?*

(The Siegfried Line was the German last line of defense, just as the Maginot Line was the French final defense line and the English Channel was Britain's last line of defense.)

At the end of May 1940, those troops who had not already surrendered to the Germans, found the beleaguered remnants of their regiments boxed into the northwest corner of Artois with twenty miles of English Channel on one side and twelve panzer divisions on the other. The allies' only escape route was by way of the beaches at Dunkirk.

The Grenadier Guards, part of the 340,000 BEF (British Expeditionary Force) successfully evacuated from the beaches at Dunkirk during the nine days of bloody, brutal fighting, fought a heroic rearguard action. When the call came from the Admiralty for every Englishman "to do his duty" almost one thousand rowing boats, cabin cruisers and fishing smacks sailed to the coast of France. Groups of five, ten or twenty exhausted soldiers, including French, Dutch, Belgian and Polish, were hauled aboard and returned to Folkstone or Dover. On June 4, Winston Churchill, then Prime Minister, addressed Parliament and described that phenomenal rescue as " . . .a victory in their deliverance."

The specter of a German invasion now loomed menacingly over us. Hitler's Operation Sealion (Seelöwe) was about to be executed. However, morale was high and there was the complete absence of panic. It seemed to me, a fourteen- year-old schoolboy, that the Germans didn't have a hope of ever conquering England. It just couldn't happen!

During the Sealion threat, however, a piece of German doggerel appeared in Punch Magazine in London.

*Was will ich tun wenn die Deutche kom hier*
*Un klop auf die tur von mien haus?*
*Will ich yelen sie könen nicht stehen bi emir*
*Oder will I bleib dum wie ein maus (Attributed to Giles)*

The four lines of doggerel were a challenge. What indeed would we do if and when the Germans got here? Would we fight or tell them to go away, or simply stay quiet like a mouse?

Mama had a plan of her own. With images of rape, torture and slave labor in her mind, she announced that she would poison us all, and asked my sister Margaret, a nurse at the Bristol General Hospital, to procure some painless poison. Margaret departed laughing; Pauline and I were not amused. But the thought remained. Anxiety ruled.

Next door to us lived the Bloomberg's, Bertie and Rachel, a quiet, very conservative American brother and sister who had come from Chicago in 1937. We seldom saw them, and may have greeted them on the street once or twice. In my mind everything about them became furtive. I began to suspect them of being spies. I decided to do some snooping.

It was Mr. Bloomberg who opened the door the following afternoon. "Good afternoon sir. I'm from next door. Can I do any yard work for you?" I saluted with three fingers to prove my rank.

"Why, yes, I know," he said. "Peter isn't it?

The coiffured head of Rachel Bloomberg popped around the door. "Ask him in for a cup of tea, Bertie."

The interior of their house was like them – staid and fusty. Nevertheless I kept my eyes open for any telltale signs of questionable activities – radio antennae, wires leading through the ceiling. I didn't see any.

Then Rachel opened the kitchen door and I was greeted with the screeching of a hundred or so love birds partitioned off behind a chicken wire cage that occupied half the room. No wonder they don't speak to anyone, I thought, they are probably deaf. Remaining calm as though everyone in Bristol owned a huge aviary, I asked them how many they had, what they ate, and if any could speak. As though in direct answer to my question, a blue-and-green bird clung to the wire close to me and screeched "DOWN WITH HITLER." It continued this condemnation until Rachel's wagging finger and piercing voice quieted it. "Naughty bird. Don't say that anymore."

Surprised, because the enunciation was very clear, I asked Rachel why. She replied, "just in case the Germans land here." I saw Bertie eying a caving knife by the stove.

I told Pauline about my discovery when I got home. "They're not spies I concluded, but I wonder what would happen if the Jerries do get here?" I giggled. "I wonder if they'll shoot the bird first, or the owners." Weeks later I met the Bloombergs on the street and asked them if they had managed to stop the bird from talking. Bertie shuffled his feet and allowed his sister to answer the question.

"Well actually, Peter, he escaped – flew out of the window." Neither looked me in the eye. I immediately thought, "Who killed Cock Robin?" and smiled inwardly, wondering "Who saw him die?"

Tuesday, June 15, 1940, came our first air raid. Certainly not the most ferocious, but it got our attention - jolted us out of our complacency. Prime targets in Bristol were the City and Avonmouth docks and the Bristol Aircraft Factory at Filton. The first heavy daylight raid was on Filton. My mother spent many anxious hours in an air raid shelter wondering about us. She did have a tale about one of the workers who had been caught taking pictures of the damage and was arrested as a suspected spy.

Anderson shelters were provided to all single households. Fabricated of arched corrugated steel set four feet down in the garden, they were, generally speaking, of little use as bomb shelters and usually ended up as coal bunkers or tool sheds. My mother said she would never leave the house for Mr. Churchill or Mr. Hitler.

The sounds and sights of warfare at home were unforgettable. Crouched under the staircase listening to the whistle of 500 pound bombs played havoc with our nerves (we heard them last two or three seconds before they struck). If they were attacking Avonmouth or the dock area, we heard the *CRUMP* from afar but quite often the Luftwaffe pilots would follow the River Avon up to Bristol and drop half a dozen sticks of bombs on the City of Bristol. During one of these raids, incendiary bombs set fire to the four huge grain silos on Canons Wharf. Because of the accumulated gasses, two of them exploded, hurling burning grain and associated matter far into the city setting numerous other fires. But perhaps the most frightening result of the granary fires was the forced evacuation of hundreds of thousands of rats into the city and outlying districts. One witness on the city side of the Bedminster Bridge said he saw them coming toward him like a huge flow of crude oil. In their terror, they crawled over each other between the confines of this narrow swing bridge, and when they reached King Street, at the other end of the bridge, they fled in every direction, seeking cover. By daylight the only visible trace were those rats which had died en route to their new homes, the rest were enjoying a new diet.

At least one of those rats arrived at our house. I heard it rummaging around in a closet next to the place where we collected under the stairs. Without telling my mother, because I knew she wouldn't understand, I plotted to exterminate it American style – by electrocution. I obtained a rattrap and wired the positive terminal of an accumulator to the spring loaded snap bar of the trap, and the negative terminal to the cheese holder. Without giving any further thought to amperes, joules, voltage or current, I set the ambush in our closet.

I had no reason to put off the execution and set the date for that night. There was no air raid that night. At 2:30 in the morning I heard the SNAP and a lot of commotion and squealing. Unfortunately my mother got to the closet first and had opened the door.

"What have ye done now, ye wretched boy?" Dressed in her nightie, she batted a huge cloud of smoke coming out of the closet. "Ye've set the house on fire, ye eejit."

I dived into the closet and extracted my device, rat and all still smoking from severe electrical burns. It was dead, alright, but I never thought that it would have been a Viking death. For two days my mother ranted about the stupidity of the son for whom she had provided the best available education and who apparently had gained nothing, and was, in fact, an imbecile. It took days to get rid of the smell of roast rat.

The warbling note of the warning siren came more often during the early part of 1943. One evening, the longest raid ever, we were all gathered in our favorite place listening to the sticks of bombs getting closer and closer. We knew they were getting close when Purdown Percy, our favorite anti-aircraft gun opened up. The earsplitting explosion of the four inch shell every two minutes soon had us cheering madly as the bombs got closer. Then, for the first time, we heard a new sound. A device the Germans had attached to the fins of each bomb. They called it *Gerät Jericho (Jericho Device)*. They were organ pipes! We could hear them from a height of 10,000 feet. The effect on the people of Bristol was psychologically paralyzing. The physically destructive power of the bomb was the same as the others, but hearing it for the first time was demoralizing. Like everything else in war, we got used to them.

A ten pound incendiary bomb landed in our back garden. My poor mother. She used words I would never have expected to hear from her mouth. While urging me to get water and douse it, she cursed the Germans and anyone else she could think of she didn't happen to like that day. I declined to do so knowing that pouring water on a hydrogen/magnesium missile could cause the oxygen to explode,( I had read it somewhere) so between the Germans and others, her favorite son came under heavy verbal fire.

The steady pulse of the diesel engines of the Dornier and Heinkel bombers remained with us all night – and the following two nights. On the third night of these massive attacks, a stick of five bombs landed quite close to us, shattering windows and bringing down plaster. My mother urged us all to pray. I did not because I knew that God was in no position to divert bombs dropped by the Luftwaffe away from people who prayed. The bombs would land exactly where they were supposed to. Better to pray that the anti-aircraft-gunners stayed out of the pubs and drank no beer, so that their aim might be better.

Emerging from our house the following morning, the first thing I noted was the strong, sickening smell of Amatol, German high explosive. It clung to everything. I heard that five or six houses on Purdown Road had been hit. Picking my way through the rubble, broken bricks and pieces of furniture, I came on the rescue crew. One of the houses had been demolished, the other four had been sliced right down the middle as though with a gigantic saw, revealing dressers, some with the drawers blown out, beds and bedding hanging off the edge of the floors, and clothing strewn about the neighborhood, grotesquely hanging from trees, lampposts and telephone wires. The street had been raped.

One of the rescuers, a member of the Special Constabulary, cocked his head on one side and said>'Hush! Hark, I can hear something." He indicated a section of brick wall that had fallen flat. I hung around attempting to give a hand. From under the rubble they extracted a woman holding a baby. Both were dead. Those two victims were my first taste of death. It is a one-sided battle, my soul screamed. It's not fair. I felt worthless, helpless and angry.

The Americans came to England in 1942 and on that very plot of land on Purdown Road, four Nissen Huts were erected for a battalion of black American troops. The white American troops were housed three miles away in Ashton Park, but they all came into the center of Bristol during the evening and made a big hit with the girls. They had fancy uniforms with silver stars and some even had medals – they had never been in combat. The British were very upset at the way these two sets of American forces fought each other. There seemed to be a genuine hatred between the black and the white. There were killings and some murders, and a detention camp was set up at Shepton Mallett, a village not far from Bristol, where U.S. servicemen were tried for crimes both against their own people and the British. Some were executed by hanging. It would take another three years of bitter infighting for the American soldier to realize that there really was a war going on and that it would take every man they had to fight it, before they gave the black soldier a rifle and told him to get into the front lines. The Americans appear to think along different lines than any other nation.

The bloodiest and most hateful air raid on Bristol took place one Friday in August in 1943, at nine-thirty in the morning, long after the regular attacks had dwindled to one or two a month. A single plane flying at 45,000 feet dropped a single bomb which struck a fully laden double-decker bus standing at the corner of Broadwier and Philadelphia streets. The explosion killed 147 people and set fire to several buildings. I don't remember any explanation for this tragic occurrence. I can only conclude that it was a new high altitude bomb sight being tried out, but why Bristol, so far afield?

The Battle of Britain had come and gone and now the USAAF were here in great numbers. Daily raids against mainland Germany were common. Thousand bomber raids then became a national treat – the sky became dark and the combined roar of Lancaster and B-17 bombers shook buildings to their foundations as they roared on their way to mete out destructive punishment on those who had dealt the same to us four years previously. I felt compassion for those civilians who would receive the weight of our attack, but we were at war – and they started it.

I left school in July 1943. I was seventeen. In March the following year I joined my first ship in Hull, Yorkshire, and sailed out into the Atlantic Ocean, now virtually cleared of U-Boats. During the following year of enemy activity, we in the Merchant Navy continued the global lifeline to England and Europe. Two years later the war ended, but our job continued, just as it always will in war or peace.

Merchant seamen numbering 133,000 were killed during WWII, most of them in the North Atlantic. My own company, a famous Liverpool steamship line, lost twenty-six ships. The nation did not mourn their loss at that time. It was sixty years that the government recognized their value. While the armed forces fought their way to victory, the Merchant Navy kept the nation alive.

*

# The Stampede

## *Adventures up the River Congo*

A wet, salty breeze off a heaving North Atlantic swell stung my face as I peered over the bridge dodger into the pitch blackness of my first night on watch. For the first time I knew that gut fear of being stalked by an invisible but all- seeing enemy. There were seventy-nine other ships out there, most of which had made up ten knot Convoy HE-190 in the Firth of Clyde five days ago. Others had joined off Northern Ireland. There was a ship six hundred feet ahead of us, another six-hundred feet on our starboard beam, yet another the same distance astern, none of which I could see. I knew, however, that there was nothing but ocean on our port side – our position was sixth ship astern of the lead ship on the outside (southernmost) column of ten ships. My job was to keep my eyes open for U-boats – periscopes or torpedo tracks. At the age of seventeen, I took my job seriously, never once giving my eyes a rest from the 7 by 50 binoculars crammed into my eye sockets, until the pain in my frontal-lobe became unbearable.

Thirty-three thousand British sailors had lost their lives in that treacherous ocean before Azdic had been perfected. Admiral Doenitz' wolf packs had lain in wait almost unhampered waiting for the eastbound/westbound convoys filled with war supplies from the United States. The only strategies the Admiralty had at its' disposal were the zig-zag maneuver and leaking false information to the enemy regarding convoy sailing times, routes and sizes. In 1943, a British submarine took on a crippled U-boat on the surface in the North Atlantic, and captured it. In the Kapitan's quarters, the Brits found an "Enigma" de-coding machine. Enigma was the top-secret code by which the

Nazi's communicated strategic naval maneuvers to their U-boat commanders. What a prize! That find evened out the playing field. The allies slowly but surely defeated the U-boat at his own game.

*Calumet*, a ten thousand ton general cargo merchant ship built in 1926, was my first ship. I joined her in Hull, Yorkshire on March 3, 1944 as a very green seventeen-year-old apprentice. After a brief gunnery course at nearby Spurn Head , we sailed northward, around the north of Scotland, through The Minches, a dangerous cauldron of water, and southward toward Glasgow and Oban, our convoy assembly port. We experienced some major damage en route, and did not finally sail until April.

Eighty ships in all sailed on a blustery April day, north and west toward the north coast of Ireland, then along the 54th parallel until reaching the 20th meridian, when forty or so ships continued westward toward the United States, the rest, including *Calumet,* altered course due south, making their various ways to Gibraltar and the Mediterranean, West and South Africa.

Leaving the Azores far to the west, we passed the brightly lit Canary Islands at night and wondered when the last German submarine had stopped there for bunkers. Off the coast of Senegal, we left the main body of the convoy and headed closer inshore, arriving at the anti-submarine barrier across the entrance to Freetown Harbor, Sierra Leone at daybreak. Perhaps fifty grey-painted ships lay at anchor within the harbor limits of the Rokel River There were no dock facilities for large ships in 1944

My first sight of Africa did not thrill me. It was heavily overcast with 99 percent humidity. I saw no monkeys frolicking in the coconut trees, and the air was filled with ghastly smells. Those impressions soon were forgotten. Under the jaundiced eye of Griff Rowlands, the bosun, we apprentices were hard at work in no time at all chipping rust off fish plates, selected sections of the upper deck; or soogeeing (washing) the paintwork with warm water and soda, a seemingly endless, boring task which always became a frenzied activity just before the ship arrived in port.

Getting out of Freetown was as much bother as getting in. Not prepared to swing the anti-submarine boom back and forth at the whim of every merchant ship, the Admiralty set times to suit themselves.

Therefore, in the company of twelve or so other ships, we steamed out of Freetown harbor at 08:00, the designated time, three days after we had arrived.

Warned about at least one U-Boat and one Italian submarines, we eased our way along the West African coast, anchoring in Accra (Gold Coast) and Cotonou (Ivory Coast) to load cocoa beans and ground nuts, working as long as daylight lasted, then shifting out of the loom of the township lights after dark for fear that we would be etched into the skyline, a perfect target for the lurking U-boat.

Our final southbound port was Matadi, eighty miles up the River Congo, in what was then the Belgian Congo (now Democratic Republic of Congo). My first sight of the river was 300 miles out in the Atlantic where a vast muddy ooze, covering hundreds of square miles, discolored the blue ocean. The egress from the Congo is so voluminous that the current has gouged a 400-foot-deep cavity into the ocean bed. At its mouth, the river is ten miles wide, at Matadi it is one mile and a half.

A few miles below the city of Matadi, under towering cliffs, there is a right-angled turn in the river which diverts part of the fastest part of the navigable stream into a maelstrom. This whirlpool is sporadic inasmuch as it takes time to build up full sub-aquatic forces to start the huge volume of water rotating.

As we approached this particular bend in the river, I remember gazing out to port, watching the upwelling as it lazily swept on down. Then quite suddenly it took on a different form. The surface of the river appeared to assume a slight dip and the whole area started to rotate. I heard the engines being rung ahead at full speed and watched the vessels' head swing to starboard, away from the swirl, steady up, then swing rapidly the other way. I had terrifying visions of being sucked in and going down bow first to the depths of that mysterious and powerful river. The efforts and local knowledge of the Belgian pilot saw us through and we docked safe and sound an hour later.

The Port of Matadi is hewn out of a single enormous granite slab which towers above the wharf, cut horizontally twenty feet above the mean river level. In those days, the engineers were working on extending the facilities; it now can berth four ocean-going ships.

After seven months confined to the ship, we were a little more than happy to have been granted the evening ashore. All spruced up in our No.10s (white tropical uniform) we looked the picture of English dignified innocence on our way up the hill toward *L'Hotel Metropole*, where I was about to get a revelation. We all ordered a litre of Congo beer, the local brew, and were halfway through the second bottle when I knew something was wrong. My world had got smaller and was beginning to whirl around. Gingerly I made my way toward the swimming pool area where I intended dipping my head in, hoping for instant steadiness. Of course, I fell in fully suited. Following all basic immediate reactions, I took my clothes off in order to wring them out, and was in the process of doing so when one of the bath attendants, a female, spotted me and started screaming at the top of her voice, *"Mon Dieu, cet un home nu! Un Anglais sans pantaloon. Salaud ! Cochon ! Allez vite »*

The patio erupted into babel. A few chairs were knocked over, and while I tried to cover up my nether parts and put my pants on at the same time, I heard women tittering behind hands, my brave companions fled.

I joined them at the bottom of the hill where many natives were displaying their wares, zebra tails, crocodile bags and highly colored cloth.

Still full of Congo beer, one of us mindlessly suggested that we allow some long horned native cattle stowed on the foredeck of a local cattle carrier, to go free.

Unbolting the bulwark gates, we drove about twenty head of African longhorn st eers off the ship onto the dock where they milled around creating consternation among the locals, and finally, a portent of inevitable disaster for us.

Our Third Mate broke up the party, ordering us back to the ship.

"Not much I can do for you lads," he explained, "It's out of my hands now. I have had to report it in the Night Log."

It was our friend the Bosun, Griff Rowlands, waking us up a few hours later who told us the good news.

"Cor blimey" he said with a certain merriment, "Wot 'ave you boys bin up to 'smorning,Eh? The Mate wants ter see yer at 7 sharp, an' I believe the Skipper does too."

The Captain saw us all on our way up to see the First Mate. "Here, you four buggers. I want a word with you before the mate gets to you. He has something quite different up his sleeve."

We trooped into the Captain's cabin and stood like schoolboys. "I might report this incident to the Head Office – what do you think of that?" Silence.

"Even drunk, it was a stupid thing to do. The Mayor, Chief of Police, the owner of the cattle . . ." He paused to let it sink in. 'They have all lodged complaints. Get out of here and see what the Mate has in store."

"Silly sods." was the Mate's contribution. "Now I want you, Peters (the senior apprentice) to organize a bucket gang with a 2" hauling line. Two of you will go into the 'tween deck and the other two into the orlop deck (the deck below). I want you to transfer as much Manganese Ore, from the orlop deck to the tween deck as you can by six o'clock this evening. Questions?"

Peters asked "What happened, sir?"

"Never mind what happened. Now get along. There will be no lunch for you today."

Manganese Ore, as its name suggests is concentrated Manganese slurry and very heavy – about one cubic foot weighs about 50lbs. A bucketful, about 200lbs.

The reader will imagine what hauling 200 lbs eight feet every two minutes for eleven hours can do to the seventeen or eighteen year old human frame. Our muscles took on a hardness that was paralyzing and our hands became like Griff Rowlands', our Bosun, in a few hours - torn and calloused.

What we did not know was the extent of the artfulness of the mate in covering up his own negligence by using our wrongdoings as justification. It appears that prior to loading the manganese ore into the 'tween deck, the mate had neglected to blank off the spaces in between the frames in way of the ships' side plating, thereby leaving an open space through which the ore poured freely into the deck below. Without so much as a "sorry lads" he had partially solved his own problem. Of the several tons of ore that found its way into the orlop deck, we only hauled up at most, a couple of tons.

We bore no malice toward the mate for we had a couple of good friends in Captain Flowerdew and Mr. Cleator. We never heard about the cattle incident again. Nor did we get any more shore leave!

# Two African Queens

## *"Only a Look and a Voice, then Darkness again, and a Silence."*

Long before you saw them you knew they were coming. High above the mangrove swamp along the banks of the Bonny River, great clouds of black smoke drifted in the Nigerian air, heralding the approach of one of Elder Dempster Line's latest acquisitions. Purchased not for their beauty but for their flat-bottomed usefulness, Oxford and Knowlton had been reprieved from noble sacrifice on the Normandy beaches, and put to work hauling coal up and down the tortuous creeks of West Africa. As they came into view around a distant bend in the river, a hoarse, bronchial blast from a highly polished brass whistle proclaimed that *this was their river.* Then, graciously slowing down at a creek side village so that houses on stilts and canoes attached thereto would not be sucked into mid-river, they sidled by before resuming their busy way toward the Gulf of Guinea and Lagos.

Built a year apart in the post-WW I Depression years, one in Quebec in 1922, the other a year later in Sunderland, England, both ships were designed exclusively for the carriage of bulk cargoes on the Great Lakes. With the bridge perched on the forecastle head, and a bowsprit-like pole extending forty feet forward by which to measure the speed at which the ship was swinging when altering course, and a tall, thin Willie Woodbine funnel atop the engine room aft, neither of these ladies could be described as graceful or attractive. Economic products of near-bankrupt shipyards hungry for business, both were constructed to owner's specifications with no allowance for frills. Their job was to haul grain, iron ore, coal or whatever was offered, and eventually to earn enough to amortize the loan taken out for their construction. With freight rates at that time on bulk cargoes mere pennies a ton, their future looked bleak and arduous.

Built at Three Rivers, Quebec in 1922 by Fraser Brace, Ltd., and named N.H.Botsford by her first owners, George Hall & Shipping Corp of Montreal, Quebec, the older ship was sold to Canada Steamships, Montreal in 1926, and re-named Knowlton, a name she bore until her end twenty-eight years later.

A year later, in 1923, the other vessel was built on the famous blocks of Swan Hunter and Wigham, Richardson Ltd, Sunderland, England to the order of The Glen Line, Ltd., Montreal, Quebec. Upon delivery she was names Glenorvie. In 1926, she too was sold to Canada Steamships. Montreal, Quebec and renamed Oxford.

Both ships were almost the same in construction and design, and each was installed with similar propulsion machinery, that is to say, each was two hundred and fifty feet in length, had a carrying capacity of about fourteen hundred tons and each traveled at eight knots.

Great Lakes vessels, although not at the mercy of a constantly heaving ocean and the corrosive effects of salt water, get their fair share of daily buffeting from numerous physical contacts with lock walls and docksides, which ocean-going ships only encounter at the beginning and end of much longer voyages. Wrinkles appear in the shell plating, particularly between the frames. As the years go by, some of these accumulated indentations get put on the "deferred repair" list, most of them in fact. Only the more serious deficiencies receive attention.

Each year, every ship classified as a seaworthy vessel with a reputable Classification Society, Lloyds or Bureau Veritas, undergoes an annual survey, known in the vernacular as a "haircut and shave." This survey is carried out to ensure that the ship is truly seaworthy, and that no major deficiencies have slipped between the cracks. The quadrennial survey, which under certain circumstances may be extended by a year, is where major repairs, and those long outstanding deferred repairs considered by the surveyor to have become embarrassing, are undertaken. The cost of these repairs escalates every four years until serious consideration is given by the owner whether to sell the ship or otherwise get rid of her.

In 1939, the older vessel entered her seventeenth year of continuous service. The other vessel, albeit a year younger, together with her sister entered drydock for their fourth quadrennial survey. Each of them was showing her age.

Notwithstanding the excellent care and maintenance taken by the crews of these aging ships, owners had some serious doubts about their future value. In 1943, the year of their next quadrennial, their fate would be decided. However, serendipity took a hand in matters and completely changed their destinies.

*

The meticulous planning that went into the Allied landings on the beaches at Normandy started as early as 1942, and culminated on June 6, 1944. Among the most serious of considerations of the Allied planners was how to keep the invading forces continuously supplied with ammunition, food, fuel – and more troops--without access to a port: for until Cherbourg and Le Havre, the two French port close to the chosen invasion sites, had been captured, it became increasingly self-evident that a jury-rigged port would have to be built right on the beaches.

To this end, huge ballasted, concrete, quay-like caissons were manufactured. In two hundred foot sections, these would be towed across the channel to act as floating docks. The next question was how to keep them shore-bound. Concrete anchors! Huge kedge anchors! were suggested. How about a 2000 ton. ship with enough explosive to blow the bottom off? Run her up on the beach – boom! You have a solid mooring.

*

Toward the end of 1942, Canada Steamships in Montreal, and several other small Lakes companies received top secret requests from the Ministry of War Transport for the use of a couple of their smaller steamers "for the duration." No details were given as to their actual intended use. Without shedding many tears, Canada Steamships gladly accepted whatever the British Government had offered and immediately set to work to prepare Oxford and Knowlton for a trans-Atlantic voyage.

Stripped of some unnecessary machinery and carrying extra bunker coal to accommodate the distance and bad weather, these two old dears transited the Lachines lock into the St.Lawrence River and started the long voyage to England. Once clear of the Strait of Belle Isle, they headed south toward Halifax, Nova Scotia, to join an eastbound convoy. Mystery mini-ships amid a convoy of eighty, 10,000 ton merchant ships all laden with wartime goods for the embattled shores of Great Britain, they became a source of concern to the commodore of one of the rare seven-and- a-half knot convoys. While under way during the fierce equinoctial gales, the Commodore lost sight of them in the Atlantic swells more times than he could see them, and when he couldn't see them, they made themselves visible by emitting huge plumes of smoke from their skinny funnels.

Struggling with the elements for twelve miserable days, and only twelve hundred feet apart, **Oxford** and **Knowlton** wondered why they were being singled out for "smoking" too much, and worn out adjusting the engine revolutions, *two up – four down*, every few minutes to stay on station. Perhaps because of their time in the Great Lakes, they were unaware that falling astern of the convoy was a certain invitation for a torpedo. Within hours of each other, both ships arrived in Falmouth on the south coast of England late in October and moored side-by-side in those centuries old docks. Under the surface, Britain seethed with pre-invasion activity.

Finally stripped of all their valuables, **Oxford** and **Knowlton** were prepared for noble sacrifice. The plan for them was to steam to an appointed place near Arromanches-les-Bains, a small coastal village halfway between Le Havre and the Cherbourg peninsula, and there run up onto the beach, detonate the small but lethal charges placed strategically below the water line the length of the ship, and hope that with the hulls resting firmly on the bottom and semi submerged they would form a rampart – a bastion – against which the floating concrete caissons, now named Mullbery, could be secured.

Perhaps because Caen was captured on July 11,1944, and Cherbourg on July 22,1944, only six weeks after D-Day, or perhaps because the weather, so foul that it may have been considered fruitless to continue with Mullbery, neither ship was called to action. They were still there in Falmouth on May 8th, V-EDAY, holding hands and wondering what all the fuss was about.

Of the 574 merchant ships lost to enemy action during World War II, twenty-six belonged to Elder Dempster Lines of Liverpool, pioneers of the West African trade.

Departing from their traditional rigid liner service, the company had discovered that an intercoastal feeder service from the creeks of the Niger, Bonny and Forcados Rivers to main distribution ports on the Atlantic coast might be a cost cutting, if not profitable business. Even though their own liners could reach inland ports such as Port Harcourt, Warri, Sapele and Burutu many miles from the Atlantic, the tonnages they could load were limited by draft restrictions by sand bars at the estuary. *Oh, for some smaller, shallow-drafted ships!*

Like waifs up for adoption, **Oxford** and **Knowlton** were inspected by several buyers (and a scrap dealer or two), and in October 1946, were purchased by Elder Dempster Lines for a restitution price of £5000 each. Ideally constructed, not only for navigation in confined waters, but for easy loading and trimming into a single hold, both vessels could cross all the bars fully laden.

Their arrival on the West Coast caused some raised eyebrows, especially among the local Empire Builders who had never seen a ship so constructed. *Why is the bridge on the forecastle head? Because the captain is always first into port.* Many thought that that was the right answer.

Dolled up in new colors, especially the tall funnel painted buff (yellow) with a dazzling brass whistle attached, and the company house flag proudly flying at the truck, these rejuvenated old dears went to work hauling coal from Port Harcourt to Lagos, Nigeria, Takoradi and Sekondi, Ghana (Gold Coast). During the next four years well over half a million tons of coal were delivered to various interest in Sierra Leone, Liberia, the Gold Coast and Nigeria; mainly however, to the Nigerian Railway.

But time was running out for these two workhorses. Perhaps the discovery of oil in Nigeria and other places along the Guinea Coast sounded their death knell, but in reality it was simply Father Time and the filthy lucre. Their seventh special survey was due in 1951, twenty-nine years after their launching. Sadly, they were not worth the expense of installing mandatory new equipment. Rust-streaked, tired, and showing it, these Amazons accepted defeat.

Oxford, the first to go, was offered for sale on the London Market on an *"as is, where is"* basis. The silence of disinterest was as ominously loud as a death sentence. Each day afloat cost the owners her daily upkeep, no matter how small. She was now a burden.

One overcast day in November, 1950, at the dockyard in Lagos, dismantled and worthless and watched by a few saddened workers, Oxford was towed down the lagoon between the breakwaters and out sea. Twenty miles south east of the port, two small charges were activated and she sank in one thousand feet of water.

The older sister, Knowlton, tendered for sale in the same manner late that same year, met a less noble but more profitable end. Sold to Thomas W. Ward, ship breakers of Milford Haven, South Wales, she was towed to her destruction in July, 1951.

*Author's note: Long after the grand new passenger liners have been converted into hotels off Greece or the North African coast, and those soulless cubic monsters, which cross the Pacific Ocean in five days carrying 600 containers have been written off after their third quadrennial survey,* **Oxford and Knowlton** *will be remembered as two humble vessels constructed and maintained with care and attention. I mourn the passing of these ships and others like them – and the men who sailed them.*

\*\*\*

# Pari Evans' Last Voyage

## *"By this leek, I will most horribly Revenge"*

*Nothing has ever unnerved me as the events of Voyage #66 in June of 1954. Apart from uncomfortable ships and unpalatable food, mostly a sailor has to deal with God's handiwork, storms, icebergs and fog. He can endure the one group of aspects and deal with the other, but when the Devil interferes, all hell breaks loose.*

I had recently been posted as chief officer of *Perseus,* a comfortable old ship, one of seven similar ships on a liner service between Bristol and the United States' east coast. We normally called at New York, Philadelphia, Baltimore and Norfolk, roundtrip voyages that lasted fourteen weeks. You can imagine, therefore, that local seafarers, officers and men preferred these vessels because of the relatively short voyages. As a result, the owners were able to select the best of the bunch. It came as both a surprise and a disappointment to the captain and to me when the superintendent announced that our regular second mate had been suddenly taken ill and there was no stand-by second mate to replace him. We would, nevertheless, sail on time and pick up a second mate supplied by the Merchant Navy Officers Pool in Swansea, South Wales., where we were due the next evening to load tinplate. A Pool officer? Unheard of. Officers supplied by the Pool were usually those who had just obtained their certificates or had not yet signed a contract with a shipping company. Some of them were good, some were downright bad. The super also announced, almost by he way, that our regular radio operator had also gone missing. A replacement would arrive before we left Bristol.

The new radio operator, nicknamed Sparks, appeared outside the captain's cabin just in time to sign on before we sailed. He had no luggage other than a small suitcase. Little man, neatly dressed in a black suit, shiny black hair brushed straight back. I found his piercing black eyes disturbing – like a cockroach, I thought.

⁜

Across in Wales, sixty miles west of Bristol, a Pool officer was telling his mates of his good fortune.

"Well, boyo's, got myself a nice berth in a swanky ship, so I have. One of them Bristol Liners." Pari Evans' shrill voice, with its somewhat grating South Wales accent, carried across the public bar of The Griffin, the main edifice on the corner of Bridge Street and The Hayes in Cardiff. "They asked for me special like," he went on after draining the tankard of India Pale ale and pushing it across the bar for a refill. "I expect they want a really good man in those ships; regular posh 'uns. Uniforms and all." He giggled. "I've never 'ad a uniform. Never likely to, neither. Whatya think, Taffy, eh?" He nudged one of his cronies, spilling his beer.

"Look out, Pari. Wotcha expect me to say." Taffy paused a moment, wondering if he dared say what was on his mind. Pari Evans could be a nasty bugger when he wanted. Taffy always kept on the right side of him. "I don't think they'll be very 'appy about you not 'avin a uniform. But then, I expect you'll tell 'em where to get off."

Evans sat for a moment, ruminating briefly on his recent ascent to the rank of second officer. He'd spent four years as deck boy on tramp steamers before scraping up enough money for tuition at Cardiff Tech. Quick to grasp the finer points of trig and algebra, he had passed for second mate a year ago. Hauling grain from Montevideo, Uruguay, did not excite him so he declined the next tramping voyage. And look what he landed!

"Your old lady is goin' to be upset, ain't she?" said Evan Williams another of Pari's hangers-on. "Leavin' her for three, four months at a time, she'll be lonely."

"Just so long as you keeps your 'ands off my Doris she'll be alright."
There was no mistaking the menace in Pari Evans' voice.

Early the following morning, Evans took the train down to
Swansea.

*

Swansea never had been one of my favorite ports of call. *Drab* adequately
described both the city and the dock area. As I scanned the expanse of
quayside and the warehouse fronting for signs of our new second mate, I
hoped only that he would fit in with our tight little Bristol group. I also
hoped he'd make it before five that evening when we were due to sail.
All I could see were the linesmen and a scruffy little fat man with his
bottom propped on the crossbar of a bicycle. Must be the agent or a ship
chandler's runner hoping to drum up a bit of business, I thought.

As we approached the dock, the fat man with a bicycle had moved
to the dock edge and propped his machine against a hydraulic crane.
Dressed in a crumpled tweed jacket and greasy grey pants, both too
small for his upper and lower girths, he resembled a comic caricature
straight off Brighton Pier.

"Hey, Mr. Mate, where are we bound and when do we sail?"

"Are you our substitute second mate?" I said, my heart sinking.

He looked at me for a second or two, "Yes, I am. Pari Evans by
name," he shouted back.

"We're bound for New York, Philly and Baltimore. Is that all the
luggage you have?" I indicated a small suitcase next to him.

"That's it," He said. "Always travel light."

*

Mr. Evans signed the ship's articles after we had docked and declined
my offer of a late breakfast saying that he was trying to lose weight.

"Good idea, Mr. Evans. By the way, where is your uniform? We
still keep the old traditions going in the Bristol Line."

Without giving me a glance, he said that he didn't have one and
never did have one. Where he'd sailed before, it was apparently of no
importance how the mates dressed.

"Is that all you have to wear?"

"Yes, Mr. Mate, and if it doesn't suit you, it's too bloody bad."

This man is going to be trouble, I thought, and decided to put him in his place.

."Your station is aft, Mr. Evans. We are loading tin plate into No.4 'tween deck. Be sure they stow the cargo properly."

"I know what I'm doing, mister, and I know when to do it." Now I loathed this man.

I waited awhile watching him, then went up to see Captain John Johnson.

"What do you make of him, John?"

"You mean our model officer?" The captain grinned. "Who did you expect, Prince Philip?

We talked about Mr. Evans for a minute or two. "Keep a sharp eye on that man, Peter, I'm afraid this is the beginning of a bad voyage." I was turning to leave when the captain held up his hand. "That new Sparks, have you met him? He's weird. There's something strange about him. Can't quite put my finger on it "

Little did we know that our nightmare had not yet begun.

*

Having already experienced his rudeness and insubordination, I had few expectations about the conduct of our new second mate at sea, but was pleasantly surprised to find that he was never late on watch, and that when he turned the ship over to me at four o'clock each morning and afternoon, he did it professionally. His behavior in the dining saloon, however, was reminiscent of a prison mess room. His high pitched voice dominated the air space, his table manners were elemental, and after a few days he began to smell. It also became obvious that he and Sparks were in conflict. The cause was not immediately apparent.

The radio operator had signed on board under the name of Patrick Burke before we left Bristol. He didn't look like an Irishman, or English for that matter. Italian perhaps. Not obliged to keep watch while the ship was coastwise, nobody had seen him until the first day out from Swansea when he turned up for lunch. He explained that he was a light eater and confined his intake to one meal a day – lunch. He sat next to Evans at the dining table. On reflection a couple of days later, I wondered who was victimizing whom. There were plenty of vacant seats in the saloon, but Sparks always chose to sit next to Evans, and Evans always sought out Sparks.

During the first four days out, several unpleasant and rather childish incidents took place at the midday meal. Evans would reach across Sparks to get the salt and in doing so would either drop the salt cellar into Sparks' soup, or jostle his arm causing him to spill his food. Each incident was accompanied by Evans' ribald comments.

"Excuse me, Sparks, while I get the salt . . . there, you've gone and done it, Sparks. You nudged my elbow; it's all your fault," and then resumed the loud monologue about some incident which had occurred down in the River Plate when he was tramping.

It was one of Sparks' dining eccentricities that brought the table baiting to an end. After taking his place, he had a habit of delicately picking up his napkin between forefinger and thumb, flicking it as though it were a whip, and deftly placing the then unfolded linen across his knee. The action never failed to bring a titter from those seated around him, a mild round of applause from the other officers, and what might be described as a malevolent smirk from Sparks.

We were making good time on the three thousand mile voyage across the North Atlantic. Although I was pleased that so far we had had no bad weather, I felt impending disaster in my bones and expressed my fears to the captain

"John, do you think that the second mate is a *Jonah*?"

"Do you mean a sailor who is a bad omen? No I don't. Do you?"

"I have to tell you that I'm not too happy about this . . .this . . . vendetta between Sparks and Evans. I sense some kind of a setup. Why don't they sit at separate tables?"

"I've seen this kind of thing before, especially with radio operators. You know the old war between deck officers and engineers – oil and water not mixing – well it's much the same with Sparks. He is only on board because of radio telegraphy; he has no other useful function." He looked at me quizzically. "But I kind of know what you're saying just the same. Be sure and let me know if either of them play any silly-buggers."

At lunch the following day, Sparks sat down and performed his napkin ritual, but as he got his napkin eye-high and gave it the usual wrist flip, he flung it in the air and let out a demonic squeak – someone had inserted an ounce or two of pepper between the folds of the linen.

That eye-smarting condiment filled the air and cleared the table. Amid the pandemonium, Evans yelled at Sparks, "That'll stop your farting in church, you nasty sod."

When the bedlam had subsided, Sparks had left. Evans sat stuffing his face as though nothing had happened.

Sitting at the head of the table, Captain Johnson kept his dignity, but I've never seen him so angry.

"Keep quiet, Mr. Evans. Kindly stop eating and pay attention to what I'm going to say." Evans, mouth open in insolent obedience, glared at the captain.

"You will arrange with the third mate to stagger your watch relief so that you and the radio operator are not obliged to eat at the same time. Is that understood?" Evans wiped his mouth and moved to leave the dining saloon.

"Don't make an enemy out of me, Mr. Evans. Did you hear what I said?" The captain concluded. Evans barely nodded and made his way back onto the bridge.

*

That evening, just as I was thinking of turning in, someone knocked on my door. It was Sparks. Of all the people on board I didn't want to see, Sparks was he.

"What is it, Sparks," I said rudely. "Aren't you supposed to be on watch?" I didn't know when his watches were – I didn't care. I just wanted to get rid of him.

"Sir, may I come in, I've something interesting you may want to hear." I opened the door wider. "Come on. Sit over there"

"I'll just stand if you don't mind."

"Did you know that the second mate reads all my traffic?" he said. The information was delivered with a certain obscure significance. "He comes into my radio shack every night and reads the imprints on the carbon paper." He stopped talking and fixed me with a snake-like gaze.

Although the news was startling, I had no intention of starting an investigation at nine o'clock at night.

"What do you want me to do about it, Sparks? I'm just about to turn in. You can do one of two things: don't throw the carbon copies in the waste basket, or lock the radio shack up    simple."

"Well, sir, it's not as simple as that. You know the Official Secrets Act?" I nodded, "Well, he's violated them and ought to be punished." Oh God. I thought. This little sod is only out for revenge. He doesn't care about the O.S.A, he just wants Evans to get into as much shit as possible. "You don't have to do anything, sir; I think I can take care of it."

"What do you mean, *take care of it?*" Sounded sinister to me. Sparks got up and edged toward the door. "It'll be alright, sir." And he was gone.

I didn't sleep very well, and made a point of banging on Sparks' door after I'd left the bridge at eight o'clock the following morning. "Let me in on your solution Sparks. What have you done?" Sparks always looked the same, morning noon and night. I wondered if he ever slept. He went into the radio shack and returned with a message "flimsy." It read:

**Master Perseus**
**Pari Evans, believed sailing on your ship as second mate, wanted for questioning in connection with homicide in Cardiff June 6, 1954. Detain on arrival New York.**

**Interpol and CID. will attend on board.**

**Signed: South Wales Constabulary.**

I had to read the message twice before it dawned on me; this was pretty sick.

"Good God, Sparks, this is not funny. Has he read it yet?"

"Who, the captain?"

"No, you bloody idiot, the second mate."

"Oh, I expect so. After all, I wrote it before I went off watch last night." Sparks wore what I could only describe as a slight leer. "You'll see," he went on, "it'll all work out in the end."

"What precisely do you mean by that, Sparks, and how far will you take this? I understand your . . . er . . . problem with the second mate, but don't you think this is going too far?"

Again that demonic look. "No sir, I don't think you really do know how his hostile behavior has stressed me." He turned to go.

Stressed him! What the hell does he mean by that? Not wishing to continue this strange conversation, I ended by telling him that I expected the joke to end before we picked up the New York pilot, seventy two hours away.

The following three days were agonizing. I think I suffered emotionally as much as Evans. At times I felt sorry for him and almost told him what was going on, and then a memory of him at his worst dispelled my weakness. The radio operator, on the other hand, seemed to be feeding off the situation. Sitting next to Evans' empty chair at the dining table, he oozed a sort of unctuous smugness. He seldom spoke, and seemed to shun any form of conversation. As for our second mate, he became noticeably thinner overnight. He answered no questions as to his wellbeing. I doubt that the punishment meted out by Her Majesty's government for infracting the Official Secrets Act would have been nearly as severe as that meted out to him by a shipmate.

On several occasions the captain asked me what was going on with the second mate. I regret that I lied to him and said that he and Sparks had apparently made some kind of truce, and had agreed to steer clear of each other. "Strange feller," said Captain Johnson, "the weirdest I've ever sailed with. And that damned Sparks. Something . . . corrupt about him, don't you think, mate?" I heartily agreed with him but continued to keep my counsel.

\*

Shortly before we docked in New Jersey, I decided to take action and stop this sick joke from going any further.

"Sparks, where the hell are you?" I pounded on his cabin door. "Have you told him yet?" There was no answer, and the door was locked; neither was he in the radio shack. I found one of the stewards and told him to find Sparks and tell him to see me on the bridge.

"You'd better get forward, Peter. We'll be docking shortly," The captain interrupted my self-recriminations for not having taken action earlier.

"Er . . .John, I'd better . . ." I started to blurt out the story, then decided to let it go. "Never mind, I'll tell you later," and I left to tie the ship up.

*

As I left the foc'stle head after the ship was all fast, I waved to the stevedore superintendent waiting on the dock, but without the usual pleasant sense of anticipation I always had on arrival at this port. The Sparks/second mate business had become a deepening depression in the forefront of my mind. And who were those people standing under the gantry crane? A group of six individuals who definitely were not ship chandlers or ships' agents. They were too well dressed.

I had barely started to discuss the discharge program with the stevedore when an apprentice stuck his head around my door and said, "Excuse me ,sir, the captain wants to see you immediately in his cabin." Anxiety drenched me as I left my cabin.

I found a grim looking captain sitting bolt upright in his chair. "Come in, Peter. This is superintendent Williams of New Scotland Yard." I shook hands with the policeman and noticed the hard lines on his face, etched by years of criminal investigation. "And this is Chief Bartowski of Newark Homicide Division." A stocky man who looked as though he'd come through the ranks the hard way nodded curtly at me. I eyed the captain's whisky bottle.

"Help yourself, Peter, you'll need it." He paused as I poured myself out a four- fingers. "Seems we have a murderer on our hands rather a *suspected* murderer our second mate, Mr. Pari Evans."

The matter-of-fact announcement sent a chill down my spine. Confusion and anger replaced my anxiety. The captain's next incredulous utterance completely floored me.

"Seems that Scotland Yard did not send us a warning message because of the possibility that the suspect might have read the text, isn't that right, Inspector?"

"Yes. We don't get this type of investigation very often but fugitives are canny and keep their backs covered. There was the strong possibility that he could have intercepted our message."

Oh, my God, I thought, time to spill the beans. "Captain, gentlemen . . ." In as concise a manner as I could, I told them the story of the cover-up, trying to put myself in the role of an innocent accomplice.

"Are you serious, Peter?" The captain was out of his chair. "You'd better organize a search immediately." He paused. "By the way, have you seen either of them since we docked?" I confessed that I hadn't.

I told the bosun to get four sailors and search the weather deck storage spaces, the steering flat and the chain locker for the second mate and Sparks. In company with the two homicide men and the captain, we unlocked Sparks' cabin and his radio shack, an experience I shall not soon forget.

A waft of icy air greeted us as we entered Sparks' cabin. There was no odor but the chill made my flesh crawl. Nothing was out of place. There were no clothes in the wardrobe; the drawers were empty. No signs of human habitation. An examination of the radio shack revealed a similar story-- neat and tidy and no evidence to show that anyone had recently been inside. The wastepaper basket was empty!

"Good God," said the Scotland Yard man, "are you sure that you actually did have a Sparks on board?" Bartowski simply said, "A fuckin' wild goose chase." The captain and I looked at each other with disbelief.

"Let's take a look in the second mate's room," I said.

It, too, was empty, but unlike Sparks' cabin, Evans had left behind his own epitaph – a chair turned over, clothes strewn across the deck – a memory of terrified haste.

*

The bos'un found the second mate in the steering flat, aft. His back was arched against the hydraulic ram of the steering engine. One knee was drawn up against his chest, both arms outstretched as though warding something off, but the horror of it all was his mouth and eyes – both wide open as if in a moment of horror-stricken denial. His fingernails were bloody. There were otherwise no significant wounds on his lifeless body.

*

While the two detectives went about the business they knew well, the captain and I sat in his cabin almost stupefied by this unimaginable turn of events.

"Why don't you get out their discharge books and see if there was anything we missed ten days ago." My suggestion at least broke the silence.

"Pari Evans' book seems to be in order," the captain said eventually. "There are no remarks in the conduct column, but the individual who signed on in Bristol as Sparks was not this Patrick Murphy. Look." He handed me the small book every seaman has showing the sequences of his voyages. Gazing from inside the front cover was the photograph of a ginger-haired man in his late fifties – Patrick Murphy. "I simply didn't compare the photograph with the bearer when he signed on," he confessed, and fell silent.

Detectives Williams and Bartowski collected evidence and conducted a thorough on-board investigation of each crew member, including the captain and me. They knew that there had been a conspiracy to terrorize the second mate, but how did Sparks know about the murder? They were men who dealt in common sense and reality. Their investigations were inconclusive. There appeared to have been neither motive nor gain. The ME reported death by natural causes – a heart attack. A senseless, apparently unmotivated homicide.

My opinion and that of the captain however, were from a different plane. For some diabolical reason, Evans had been hexed and the forces of evil had simply taken their toll. ship owner's reaction to the news of the second mate's demise was both childish and demanding. Even after a lengthy telephone conversation with the captain, they said they needed a written report with a full explanation. From our point of view the incident was over. No amount of discussion and no library of reports could alter the fact that we had a dead body on our hands, or rather in the city morgue, and the question was "Can't those Americans bury it somewhere?" The Managing Director had asked.

"Where do you suggest, sir?"

"Oh don't be awkward, captain, in one of their cemeteries of course."

"I'm pretty sure they don't have spare plots in their graveyards for recalcitrant sailors. How about a sailor's burial at sea?

"Oh, jolly good idea, captain. How clever of you. We'd better make sure the next of kin agrees."

"There is no next of kin recorded in his discharge book."

"Then go ahead. Take some photographs – just in case."

Captain Johnson leaned back in his chair and placed both hands over his eyes. "And they run the bloody company!"

*

The captain and I declined the company's offer to send out a replacement second mate. We each felt more comfortable standing watch-and-watch (four on - four off), but a new radio operator arrived from the UK before we sailed southward.

The autopsied remains of our late second mate, swathed in a simple white hospital gown and contained in a strong, plastic receptacle, was delivered alongside a few hours before we sailed from Port Elizabeth. Without discussion it was decided to weight the box with one hundred pounds of chain, secure the lid and bury him as-is. Because of the inconstant ocean currents close inshore, we would have to wait until homeward bound from Halifax, Nova Scotia, five weeks hence. Meanwhile the *corpus delicti* was secured in an upright position in the meat locker at -20.F.

Neither Captain Johnson nor I found it easy to put the events of the past week behind us. Each of us blamed ourselves in some way for allowing sparks to leave the ship undetected. The police had placed a man on the gangway, and I had posted an AB. with instructions physically to detain the radio operator if he tried to leave the ship. Neither the policeman nor the sailor had seen him. The APB released by the Newark police bore the likeness and the physical description of the owner of the discharge book, Patrick Murphy. They would never get him!

A piece of shocking news greeted us on our arrival in Baltimore. Our new radio operator had made enquiries from Marconi about the owner of the discharge book and was advised that Patrick Murphy had been on board a ship named *Kestrel* two months ago and had died in Calcutta – of food poisoning. The mystery deepened and took on a more macabre aspect. We were homeward bound now. In eight days we'd face the British press not to mention the suspicion and criticism of the owners.

Eight hundred miles east of Halifax harbor, close to the Grand

Banks, we held a short burial service at the beginning of the eight-to-twelve watch. We had reduced speed simply for the sake of decorum. Away to the north faint shades of the *aurora borealis* were caught and reflected by a long, oily swell. With little or no enthusiasm, those members of the crew not otherwise engaged, mustered at No. two hatchway to witness the burial. It was all over in five minutes. As the plastic "coffin" sank beneath the waves, a faint scream came out of the darkness to the east, and an albatross swooped low over the water, yards from where Pari Evans had plunged to join his shipmates in Davy Jones' Locker.

*

I seldom speak of that voyage although it rarely leaves my mind for long. I am haunted by visions of that hideous face staring up at – *what?* And of the radio operator who appeared out of nowhere and disappeared in the same manner.

The old *Perseus* has gone now, gone to the knackers' yard, and I have grisly visions of parts of her being made into razor blades and someone accidentally cutting his throat.

I am master now, but no voyage ever goes by that I don't scrutinize the discharge book and passport of every radio operator. I'm just an old-fashioned sailor.

*

For a while The Griffin in Cardiff did a roaring business. Reporters from The South Wales Gazette practically lived in the place.

"Where was he sittin' then, the last time you saw 'im?"

"What were the last words you remember him sayin'?"

The questions kept coming, and Pari Evans' three cronies bathed in the spotlight. When they ran out of true facts, they invented them until the saga of Pari Evans became legend. Between themselves, however, lay the bare facts of their brief, public-house acquaintance.

"Always did think 'e was a bit of a rascal; bit of a liar too." Evan Williams sat back on his stool and looked to his chums for support.

"Do you reckon 'e did Doris in, then?" Gareth Hughes finally asked the obvious, painful question.

""Course 'e did. Who the 'ell do you think did it? The group fell into alcoholic melancholia, each gazing into the foam in his tankard for solace.

"Cor, look who has just come in? Doris' sister Mabel. Who'se that with her?" The sudden observation was enough to interrupt his companion's beer drinking. They followed Gareth's gaze to a table near the food counter where a small dapper man dressed in black suit was ushering a youngish woman into a chair.

"You're right, you know," Gareth hoarsely whispered, "but I don't know the feller; never seen 'im before."

"Looks like a bleedin' undertaker, I'd say. Bit bloody late for poor old Doris." The trio laughed coarsely.

The couple sat down, ordered a meal and then sat talking earnestly until it arrived. Then the little man did the strangest thing: he picked up his linen napkin between thumb and forefinger and jerked it open before deftly placing it across his lap!

*

# A Fortuity of Transit
## The Perils of the Sea

It was always with a form of stoic insanity that I faced yet another North Atlantic crossing. They say that the Atlantic Ocean has two seasons—nine months of winter and three months of bad weather. I had been doing it for twelve years, and I had another twelve to go.

This would be my fifth trip as first mate on *New York City*, a well-found ship of some 9000 tons gross tonnage. Next voyage I would be master, a cushier job perhaps, but with the added responsibility of the lives of forty crewmembers and the safety of the vessel itself. As first mate I was only responsible for the cargo. It was in my best interests to ensure that the cargo was stowed securely to my satisfaction before we sailed, for securing cargo at sea is never much fun. On this occasion, however, I made a "pier head jump" (joined the ship in a hurry at the last minute) and did not examine all the lashings.

Built in 1953, to Lloyds A.100 specifications, *New York City* was a medium-sized freighter of the day, and a comfortable ship even in storm force conditions. This voyage, however, she was riding light, drawing thirteen feet forward and twenty-two feet aft, a fact that probably saved my life and those of the bosun and two hands.

We headed out of the Bristol Channel into a short choppy sea under leaden skies. Rain squalls joined ocean and sky like the curtains on a vast watery stage. I groaned; the harbingers of foul weather ahead were evident. A long, low swell more than a mile from crest to crest told me that there was something big and nasty a thousand miles ahead. The barometer, 1000mb when we sailed, was now down to 979mb;

not unusual, but nonetheless significant. The coastal sea birds were swooping and screaming warnings at us as if to say, "You'll be better off a week from now." Then they vanished. We would see them again four months from now on our return journey.

Four days out, the barometer had fallen to 959mb and the wind had come around to the southeast, force seven. The synoptic chart showed a well developed low pressure system stationary in the Davis Strait, that perilous stretch of water between Greenland and Labrador, where the barometer was reported at 940mb, just under 28" of mercury. Our barograph recorded an almost vertical drop.

"We're in for a wee blow, mister mate." The captain's voice had roused me from nostalgic thoughts of sitting around the fireside, all warm and comfy.

"Yes, sir. Just as soon as this front passes, it'll get mighty cold and we'll probably have some very disagreeable weather." I looked at the captain's craggy face and was glad he was in command instead of someone I didn't know.

"I'm taking the bosun and a couple of hands on deck to tighten up the lashings on the lashings deck cargo. Watch out for me, sir."

"Aye, laddie, I'll do that for ye," and shoved his briar pipe back between his teeth, but not before cautioning me, "Careful now!"

The last cargo laden on board in Bristol had been two hundred forty-gallon steel drums containing liquid resin, each weighing about four hundred pounds. They had been stowed in a single tier on the foredeck from the forecastle head to the bridge front, alongside numbers one and two hatches. It was the lashings around these drums that I and three burly sailors spent two hours inspecting and tightening.

Two hours later I reported back to the captain that all that could be done, had been done.

The following morning, when I went on watch at 4:00 a.m., the ship was laboring heavily in a mountainous northwesterly swell. The cold front was close at hand and the wind had strengthened to hurricane force. With the barometer recording 920mb, a reading that set my heart racing the lowest I'd ever encountered, I knew we were in for a humdinger.

By 8:00 a.m., the wind had veered from west-by-north to north-north-west and had increased to force eleven. The swell had steepened. As far as the eye could see, the sides of cliff-like fifty to sixty foot swells were streaked with mile-long lines of foam. The barometer was still plummeting. The latest synoptic chart showed that a high pressure system over Quebec, contiguous with a trough of low pressure over Greenland were combining to manufacture one of the worst storms in decades—and we were now in the south-east quadrant. There was no escape; we had to grin and bear it.

Shortly after 8:00, the ship buried her nose into the middle of a great curly green sea, and almost came to a shuddering stop. Cups of tea and cocoa went flying all over the bridge. Watch keepers hung on for dear life. The engine room telephone rang. The melodious tones of our irate chief engineer's voice echoed around the wheelhouse: "What the heck are ye doing up there? The governor can't keep the main shaft under control. I'm afraid ye'll have to ease up on the revolutions or we might lose the propeller." It was thought that had already crossed my mind: when a ship encounters a heavy swell head-on, great care must be taken not to let the propeller spend too much time churning air as the stern comes out of the water. The problem facing the captain under circumstances such as this is that you must have sufficient revolutions to maintain steerage way in order to avoid "broaching to"—allowing the sea and swell to hit the ship beam-on.

We had not yet decided to heave-to, but when the welter of sea and foam had run over the foredeck back into the ocean, the captain announced that he would do so. Of the several hundred drums on deck, half had broken adrift and many had gone over the side, taking with them several sections of portable shipside rails. The remainder lay battered, dented, and leaking, wedged obscenely between the winches or piled up in a heap against the bridge front housing.

"Steer northwest, quartermaster. Reduce speed to fifty-five r.p.m., third mate."

"Aye, sir," they replied as with one voice. Laboriously the old ship came up into the weather, straining and protesting, all of her transverse and longitudinal stiffeners letting us know how well they were holding the ten-year-old vessel together.

"What do you think about that lot, mister mate?" the captain jerked his thumb toward the foredeck.

I had already given the matter some thought, and had concluded that something would have to be done before another boarding sea compounded the already existing chaos. the rest of the deck cargo got adrift, some of the winches might be destroyed, and the bridge front plating might be penetrated.

"Keep her like she is, sir, and I'll take the bosun and two hands to see what we can jettison. I'm not going to attempt to re-secure any cargo at this juncture."

The captain eyed me for a second or two. "Have a care, laddie. Buckle yere'selves up, and keep your eye on me and the weather." He jammed his pipe back between his teeth and turned away.

It was cold on deck, almost cold enough for saltwater to freeze. Oil-skinned up with heavy plastic gloves to protect our hands from frostbite, and gripping pry bars and wire cutters, we stepped out into the starboard alleyway—the side away from the weather—and began our perilous journey up the heaving deck, lifelines secure around our waists. The bosun and I took the port side while the AB's took the starboard side.

About ten minutes later, after making sure that fifty or so drums would do no further damage, I had a strange sensation that I was in another place, not in a mid-Atlantic storm but somehow—sheltered. The shrieking of the wind through the rigging had ceased, and that seething noise the sea makes when it is angry could no longer be heard. In this brief lull, I heard a faint cry and looked up at the bridge. The captain was leaning over the dodger yelling at me and pointing away over the starboard bow. I glanced to where he was pointing—and froze. A mile away, bearing down on us at forty knots, I saw a fifty foot swell just beginning to curl and break at its crest. I knew the outcome from experience. Like a Hawaiian surfer, we were about to get caught in the tunnel. Even as I yelled a warning to the other three lads on deck, I could see that they were aware of the oncoming danger. They had scampered for whatever protection was close at hand. My own actions were instinctive. I struggled as fast as I could toward the oncoming wave and hurled myself on the after side of a mast-house, pulling my safety line as tight as I could—and waited. I suppose I said some prayers, but they were really sincere hopes that if I were to be killed, it would be quickly and painlessly. I really didn't want to come out a living paraplegic.

I felt the ship shudder as the main body of water tried to move her physically from one place in the ocean to another, then the crackling roar of the crest started to cascade like a massive waterfall. All at once

I was not a quivering being waiting for the worst, but a tadpole caught up in a million gallons of wild water with the power of a hundred horses.

My cinched safety rope tightened until I thought that if it didn't part, it would cut me in half. The breath was completely knocked out of me and the extreme cold made me draw it in again, causing me to swallow a fair amount of the western ocean.

During the thirty or forty seconds I was submerged—which felt like an eternity—the real fear gripped my soul. Adrenalin had taken me swiftly to what I hoped would be a safe place; fear now was trying to undo my resolve to stay alive—it's called panic! Crouched in a semi-fetal position I could feel the main body of water rushing past me. I had to quell the instinct to stand up and fight it. I had no idea what had changed since I first took cover. Then I felt the upward surge as the ship rose under the following swell and my head emerged. I opened my eyes and gazed across a waste of ocean that appeared to be moving away from me at breakneck speed. I looked to the northwest and saw quite the opposite: a range of watery mountains bearing down on us. I heard faint cries and saw that the two sailors on the starboard side were scrambling to the safety of the alleyway and a watertight door. I found the bosun a few seconds later, stretched out on the steel deck. His lifeline had saved him from certain death. He was alive and stirring. My wristwatch was missing and my oilskin jacket had been rent from the collar to the lower hem, otherwise I was sound, but shaky.

I glanced up at the bridge and saw a slight smile on the captain's face. He was beckoning us in. I needed no encouragement. The other two lads, I guessed, were safely inside, as the bosun and I gingerly made our way, each supporting the other, toward the port alleyway—where we encountered seven or eight steel drums jammed into the entrance, creating an impassable barricade.

"We're going to have to get some of these over the side, sir," the bosun said almost apologetically. I agreed with him and grasped the nearest drum around the bottom chime and began edging it toward the upper edge of the sheer strake. I had it half over the fishplate when the ship gave one of those graceful lurches, like a drunken sailor. The center of gravity of the barrel shifted as the portside dipped further into the ocean—and away it went, with me stuck to it. With nothing to hold me—I had already discarded my lifeline—I saw the end of days looming up, glued to a steel drum of resin "I'll be joining my Dad shortly" went through my mind; he'd been drowned at sea thirty years before. But the Angel of Mercy was still hanging around. I felt two brawny arms rugby-tackle me around the waist, and I watched the drum—with my gloves still stuck to it—slip into the roiling wash and sink in two thousand fathoms.

Driven by panic and desperation, the bosun and I scrambled over the remaining drums and fell into the lower accommodation, completely exhausted.

"Close call, mister mate." A man of few words, the captain tried to express his relief in the short space of time he removed the pipe from his mouth. "Glad ye made it, laddie. I would'na have liked to keep your watch for the rest of the voyage." I really did like him, in spite of his sense of humor.

At the end of the voyage, I was obliged to explain the loss of all that cargo to the owners, so that they could satisfy underwriters. I remember writing in detail the nature and extent of the damage, but when it came to the "cause of loss," I hesitated. I could have written "heroic foolishness" or "inattention to duty," but I ended with the impenetrable, unfathomable phrase, "a fortuity of transit," and silently added, n*ever again!*

\*

# The Sharks Fin

*One of Life's Milestones.*

The marine weather forecast sounded like a fairy tale: light to moderate southeasterlies, slight seas and swells. Britain was under a dome of high pressure. That, to the coastal sailor, was a promise of smooth seas and gentle zephyrs. In other words, we could anticipate a smooth passage without the usual injury-defying clambering from bridge to cabin or saloon while the ship performed the antics of a circus acrobat.

I was mate of *Sirius,* a 1000- ton coastal steamer engaged on a liner service between the Bristol Channel and ports in Belgium and Holland. We made about twenty continental voyages each year. We knew every rock, outcrop, shoal and shoreline village from Somerset to Kent. As we passed under the Bristol Suspension Bridge on our way to sea on that April evening in 1954, I would shortly thereafter have found a few rocks and shoals whose acquaintance I would wish never to have made.

I look back at the events of the following spring day, the day after we sailed from Bristol, as one of the milestones in my life.

I came on watch at four o'clock in the afternoon feeling at peace with the world. Our little ship, at home in these waters, performed like a lady. To the west, where sea met sky, the horizon stretched like a knife's edge from north to south as far as the eye could see. Glistening wavelets dotted the cobalt ocean, giving the scene an enchanting holiday appearance. To the east, the craggy coast of Cornwall, closer than I would dared to have ventured two years ago, rose majestically. Cars were visible driving along the cliffs. Families picnicking on the rocky beaches waved; you could almost see them smiling. Ahead, fine

on the port bow, lay the Longships Lighthouse rising 140 feet above
the rocks on which it was built. Farther to the west, the sea surged over
the Seven Stones reef, graveyard to many a ship. This was Lands End!

We had passed Pendeen and the Brisons, a group of tall rocks that
lay on the port beam about four miles distant. Our present course of
SSW would take us west of the Longships by a mile-and-a-half. Why
should I not take the inside passage, the narrows between Lands End
and the Longships, and save about thirty miles, and two hours and
twenty minutes? I had seen it done twice before under the sure eye
of the captain. Keep your cool, watch for the markers – a piece of
cake. I didn't stop to consider the true reason I might take on this bold
adventure. Grandiosity perhaps? Stupidity? Not really. I had done this
before.

The conditions were just right. A strong tide was running south-
by-east through the narrows (one would never take this passage on a
flooding tide). Visibility appeared unlimited, and the sea was no more
than, slight.

I had bidden farewell to the second mate and gone into the chart
room to fix our exact position. Standing poised in the wheelhouse,
where it seemed safer than on the wing of the bridge, I had a brief
thought of those soldiers in the trenches in Flanders; "*When the whistle
blows Lads, go over the top.*" For many, the last move of their life!

"Port easy," I said to the quartermaster in as confident a manner
as I could.

"Port easy, aye." Did I detect a slight query in the quartermaster's
response?

The small ship answered the helm immediately. As I watched the
ship's head swing to port and the lighthouse disappear behind the
foremast, panic began its insidious job. *Maybe I shouldn't do this! Next
voyage, perhaps? Come on you silly bugger, Peter. It's been done a thousand
times. There's plenty of water hard against the rocks – just don't hit 'em.*

"How's your head?" I spoke quietly. My throat had become dry.

"One-eight-0h, sir."

"Steady on one-seven-five." The quartermaster repeated the
heading and steadied her up with the lighthouse fine on the starboard
bow, three miles distant too bloody late to change my mind now.

My Catholic upbringing joined in the attack on my senses. You

are committing a sin of Pride! What if you founder, I thought, you'll
be guilty of murder!

The Shark's Fin! I remembered the Captain telling me that once
you have sighted the Sharks Fin, your worries are over. I had to find
this large rock and keep it on the starboard side – between it and the
lighthouse were rocks!

Assisted by a six-knot current, *Sirius* barreled along at eighteen
knots. The slate and granite cliffs and the numerous rocky stacks that
edged the coastline as far as I could see, became a surreal blur.

The closer to the narrows we got, the faster the ship went. The sea
became confused and steep. Also a wind came from nowhere. Nothing
was clearly outlined anymore. Spume filled the air. The sea, too, had
kicked up making most of the rocks disappear under welters of foam.
A sickening fear began to undermine my resolve

"Keep your eye out for the Shark's Fin." I croaked at the
quartermaster. "Should be pretty close now, on the starboard side."

The noise too, had increased; the general background rumble
of distant surf became the roar of waves breaking on rocks. Stepping
outside the wheelhouse to get a better view of my surroundings, I
was startled to see the lighthouse towering high above me. What had
always been a friendly point of departure had now become a menacing
monument. I lowered my eyes toward its base . . . what was that? I
had glimpsed a large rock about one point before the starboard beam.
I managed to bring the binoculars to bear and to focus on . . .Yes! the
Shark's Fin!

"Starboard easy. Steady-up on one-nine-oh," I yelled, instantly
feeling the weight of the world being lifted from my shoulders. The
lighthouse, now slightly abaft the starboard beam, rapidly diminished
in size and once again became a friendly beacon. The quartermaster's
inscrutable face spoke volumes. *Don't ever do that again while I am at
the helm.*

With trembling hands I wiped the sweat from my brow and out
of my eyes, then leaned against the bridge dodger wondering why did
I ever do that?

A quiet, seemingly unperturbed voice behind me answered my
question. "Don't ever do that again without my authorization, Mr.
Wright."

I never did.

# The Coffin
## *An Irreverent burial at Sea*

*I have a hard time accepting the spiritual catholicon which suggests that we find ourselves in certain places at certain times because we are supposed to be there, or something significant happens because it was supposed to happen. I am more inclined to acknowledge the advent of sudden happening, disasters, by believing the modern, more philosophical explanation that "shit happens."*

**Rotterdam. 1953.** The familiar hustle and bustle of a ship making ready for sea always brought to mind the awakening of a grubby, untidy giant. While tied up alongside a dock, a ship is nothing but a warehouse invaded by landlubbers. The minute cargo work is completed and the crew covers and battens down the hatches, lowers the derricks and secures her for sea, she becomes alive; scrubbed down, with a clean pair of knickers on, she's is ready to go where she belongs.

Standing in my cabin looking at the activity on the foredeck, I saw the bosun, Alfred Johnson,conducting his usual pre-sailing ballet, shuffling backward on the hatch covers, his eyes skyward, directing with his arms, as an orchestra conductor might, at the sailor who was lowering the derricks into their respective crutches. I'd watched him do this a hundred times and never given it a thought. But this time I noticed that someone had left one of the hatch covers off and the bosun was shambling backward toward a four-foot by ten-foot opening which accessed the lower hold twenty feet below.

I opened my mouth to yell at him. Realizing that he couldn't hear, I picked up a paperweight and hammered on the window, all to no avail.

Completely oblivious of the gaping hole behind him, he somersaulted backwards and disappeared from view.

He was dead when I knelt by his mutilated body three minutes later. I must confess that my first thoughts were not of his wife and kids, but of the ship's schedule – we would arrive late into Plymouth! I was a company man.

The ship's agent in Rotterdam, a witness to the accident, had already called the police who threw up a barrier along the quay to ensure that none of the crew "escaped." Brushing aside my own explanation as to the cause of the tragedy, the police inspector started a homicide investigation. With the national stolidity of a nation that endures living thirty-five feet below sea level, he took statements from each crew member. Two hours later, convinced that there had been no foul play, they allowed the coroner to remove the body to the city morgue. With the help of the ship's agent I signed a document that bound me to pay all dues, fees and storage for the corpse until someone had claimed the remains and made arrangements for its disposal.

We cleared the River Maas that evening shortly after ten and set course for the Foreland. It was only when I came to write up the incident in the official log book that I gave a personal thought to the man who had been killed, bosun, Johnson, a good man when sober. Out of his meager wages of £4 a week, he allotted his wife Mary £2. He was a man who would be missed on board, but not for long. Personal attachments are not common on weekly boats. (*small coasters engaged in weekly trips between ports*).

After breakfast the following morning, I reluctantly picked up the phone to get the owner's view on the casualty.

"Hello, Bob, I expect you've heard about Johnson"

"Yes I have. I expected to hear from you," Robert Shannon, the Marine Superintendent, sharply replied.

"There wasn't enough bloody time last night." Fact is I deliberately had not called him. The day had already gone badly enough. "Did you say that his wife was on holiday in Scotland?" I continued.

"I believe in Glasgow."

"Okay. You'd better let her know as soon as you can," I told him. It was only a gentle reminder, but he took it personally

"No, I'm not telling you how to do your damned job! Good-bye!" I slammed the phone down.

Bob and I were really good friends; I'd caught him on a bad morning.

Later that day when St. Albans Head was broad on the starboard beam, the mate handed me the phone and said, "Head office."

"I spoke to Mrs. Johnson an hour ago." Bob sounded less irritated. "She was naturally very upset and wants his remains brought home. Also, she wanted to know if his allotment would continue until the end of the voyage. By the way, did he have any overtime coming to him?"

"Not much. But no, he's off the Portage Bill. His account of wages is already made up, together with the Death on Board and a list of his personal effects."

"You've some explaining to do when you meet the shipping master." There was a hint of malice in his voice.

"Bollocks," I said, and hung up.

Three days later we were in Bristol. I was still smarting from shipping master's sarcasm. "You say he was walking backwards on the hatch cover when he fell into the lower hold?"

"Don't worry about it, laddie." The marine superintendent saidBob said. "Are you going to pack the body in dry ice or keep him in the freezer?" He smirked at my discomfort.

"Don't really fancy keeping him in the freezer along with all our edible frozen commodities. Besides, he'll take up too much room. I'll probably wrap him up in a tarpaulin packed with dry ice. Should keep him from stinking, shouldn't it?"

"Don't know much about that sort of thing, your problem." Smug bastard.

The weather had turned nasty by the time we rounded The Lizard on the eastbound leg of the following voyage. We had left Swansea the evening before having loaded 1200 tons of tinplate. Stiff as a board with all that bottomweight, the ship behaved as though she had the hiccoughs. Two hours later the wind had increased to force eight out of the east and we were taking green seas on deck.

I took the proffered phone from the second mate with my right hand, my left arm being hooked around a stanchion,hanging on for dear life,

"Yes Bob. This isn't a very good time to talk. . . ."

"This is important, Peter," my superintendent interrupted me, "I just got off the phone with Mrs. Johnson. She's had a change of heart. It seems that as much as she loved her husband, she doesn't love his dead body. She wants it buried at sea, not in Holland "with all them furriners," as she put it, but in proper seagoing style."

"You want us to sew him up in a tarpaulin jacket and put the last stitch through his nose?" I thought I was being smart.

"Not at all, you saucy bugger. I have already arranged with our agent in Rotterdam to have a local coffin maker construct one of hardwood and zinc, and to have twelve one-inch inch by half-inch holes drilled around the sides. These can be plugged with suitable doweling until he gets dropped." Bob sounded selfsatisfied.

"There's no need for me to verify all of this." I hung up without waiting for an answer.

Once clear of the Foreland, the wind backed to the northwest and abated. We were two days late into Rotterdam.

The last item loaded on board was Johnson's body in an oversized coffin. Strongly built of hardwood secured around the base with quarter-inch" zinc strapping, and similarly lined, it measured six-foot by three- foot by three-foot and weighed close to 600 pounds, a veritable sarcophagus. The longshoremen placed and secured this monstrosity on a pair of trestles under the forecastle head. We sailed an hour later, not bound for Plymouth, as was planned, for someplace in the Western Approaches to the British Isles, the latitude and longitude of which I had not yet determined.

Sailors, even modern sailors, are a strange lot, me included. We went about our tasks silently, as though we were in the shadow of death itself. Superstitious, as most West Country sailors are, they regarded this leg of the voyage as though we were "ridin' a hearse." The very mention of the deceased being on board brought up the *Jonah* curse, causing a shiver to run down every spine.

Light westerly airs barely rippled the surface of the water. The English Channel reflected a cobalt sky that stretched westwards forever. The horizon divided earth and sky like a knife edge, a good day for a burial.

At nine o'clock the owner called me.

"Good morning captain. Weather good?" A man of few words.

"Yes, sir." I would make this as short as possible.

"Let me remind you Captain, not to dawdle after you have conducted the burial service, time is money! And please take some photographs – for the widow, you know."

Somehow or other he had just ruined my day.

At four o'clock in the afternoon we were twelve miles south of the Eddystone Lighthouse, a perfect place to put to rest the body of a sailor. Admirals Nelson, Rodney and Hood had made their departures from this very spot; and in Plymouth, twenty miles due north, Sir Francis Drake calmly finished his game of bowls after being notified that the Spanish Armada was in sight.

"Stop engines. All hands to witness burial." My announcement sounded melodramatic and slightly Hollywood-ish.

"Excuse me, sir, that bleedin' coffin weighs half a ton, how are . . .?"

I interrupted him. "Don't complain to me about something you are going to do anyway! Get on with it."

Nevertheless, I winced as I watched four burly sailors emerge from the forecastle space with the coffin on their shoulders, staggering to our homemade catafalque(platform for a coffin), two wooden hatch boards, paradoxically similar to those whose absence had caused his death, placed between bulwark and hatch coaming. After the Red Ensign had been draped over the coffin, the mutterings and complaints slowly died down. All that could be heard was the faint sounds of the main generator muted by the vastness of the living ocean.

Grasping the Book of Common Prayer firmly in my hand, I climbed onto No.1 hatch to perform a ceremony I'd never done before. I noted that the carpenter and the third engineer, armed with pliers and a mallet, were ready to remove the bungs from the sides of the coffin. No longer a piece of unwanted freight, a *corpus non grata* as it were, Alfred Johnson's remains were about to join those of the brave mariners already at rest in Davy Jones' Locker.

"We therefore commit his body to the deep, to be turned into corruption, looking for the resurrection of the body when the sea shall give up her dead."

Suddenly the entire crew reeled backward clutching at throats and noses, and making gagging noises. A moment later my indignation turned to horror as the cause of their histrionics reached my nose – a most vile stench emanating from the few bungholes already cleared.

"Cut the lanyard." I yelled, "Get the bloody thing over the side before the plague breaks out."

Finally the coffin plunged into the sea and disappeared beneath the waves. Free at last, all earthly bonds untied, Mr. Johnson had joined the motley crew on the ocean floor.

Shamefacedly, some the crew dismantled our humble altar, folded the flag and shuffled off to their various duties. I too, disappointed and sad at the shabby ending to a ritual which I had hoped would afford the deceased a modicum of dignity, made my way toward the bridge. "Poor bugger," I muttered, perhaps his only eulogy.

A tug at my sleeve. "Sir, it's afloat; it's come to the surface!" The hair on the nape of my neck bristled. With unbelieving eyes I followed a pointing finger and saw what had emerged as my nemesis – four feet of one end of the coffin - bobbing and dodging about between the sparkling waves. Not without a tinge of fear I thought, he's come back to argue about his overtime.

My mind panicked. Grisly images of the interior of the coffin entered my mind. What hideous mess had prevented the water from ingress? What if it washed ashore? And what if Mrs. Johnson found out that her late husband had ended up as common garbage washed up on a Devon beach? The solution dawned on me as soon as the panic abated – it had to be sunk by any means at my disposal. I had no firearms on board. The idea of mincing it with the propeller crossed my mind. But how would I explain the inevitable chips and dents to the delicate periphery of those phosphor-bronze blades? Conclusion? I had to ram it!

I explained to the chief engineer and the first mate what I was going to do. Neither of them held out much hope for success. They suggested that we come alongside the flotsam, lower a man down armed with an axe and sink it by hand. Too dangerous: I didn't want to lose another man. They snickered at I left for the bridge. God will get you for that, I hoped.

As I turned and made the fourth run at the defiant box, a line from one of Robert Southey's poems came to mind: "Without any sound or sign of the shock, the waves broke over the Inchcape Rock."

Coming out of the maneuver, I scanned the waters on the starboard quarter. There was no sign of my nemesis. My most fervent hope was that his remains were at last where they belonged – down among the dead men and the wrecks a hundred fathoms deep.

That evening as we rounded the Longships and headed for the Bristol Channel, I made an entry in the official log book.

"Friday, June 20th,1953; 16:30. After a short memorial service, the body of A.Johnson. bosun was committed to the deep twelve miles south of the Eddystone Lighthouse without incident" and made a small act of contrition.

*Pw.*

# Part Three
## Stories Ashore

# Duty and Dedication

*"From Lightening and Tempest: from Battle and Murder, And Sudden Death, Good Lord Deliver Us."*

Book of Common Prayer.

*

*The North Atlantic Ocean has no favorites. If you parallel sail in latitude 54° N., there are certain rules of thumb derived from a general maxim to which the wise sailor will pay heed, that there is always a killer storm somewhere in that vast stretch of water.*

\*

In a small, neat house in Cheltenham, thirty-five miles north of Bristol, England, Captain Harry Dunning finished his morning cup of tea, rubbed the stubble around his chin and decided that he would shave. Looking critically at his young but worry-lined face in the bathroom mirror, he applied soap and began to shave.

"Where did you say they were going to send you this time, Harry?" Grace Dunning, his wife, appeared at the bathroom door. Receiving no immediate reply, she went on, "Was it Nova Scotia or Newfoundland or some such place?"

"St. John, New Brunswick, dear," he replied. "Not far from Halifax, but still a bloody awful place as far as I remember. Cold as charity in the winter; never gets up to 60, even in July or August."

"Since when have they been growing bananas in New Brunswick?" asked Grace Dunning sarcastically.

"Very funny," said Harry Dunning laughing. "No, we're going for a full load of frozen meat; beef probably, for Bremen and Hamburg. Those poor buggers are starving to death over there."

Dunning, master for several years of one of Elders & Fyffe's regular banana ships, trading between the West Indies and Avonmouth, had been mildly irritated at the end of his last voyage to Jamaica, when the marine superintendent told him that his next command would be that of *Empire Abbey*, a two-year old standard ship built for Royal Mail Lines, but presently under charter to the Ministry of War Transport. The MOWT was a war-time government department instituted to control the movement of all merchant ships, foreign flag included, that sailed under the British protective convoy system during WWII. In peacetime, merchant ships are controlled solely by their owners and trade along well established routes. In wartime, they were directed to sail wherever they are most needed.

He knew the North Atlantic Ocean well, but not the western ocean, the part where all the nasty weather accumulates. Of *Empire Abbey* he knew nothing except that she was a class of standard "utility" ship (signified by the prefix *"Empire")* built in 1944 to government specifications by the Shipping Corporation, Newcastle-on-Tyne (7,032 GRT) without any frills. She was fitted with five refrigerated cargo holds. Her main propulsion was an economy, five cylinder Doxford diesel engine. Presently in Avonmouth docks, she was due to sail for Canada on Monday evening, January 15, 1946.

He and Grace went to St. Mary's (Church of England) Church at 10 a.m Sunday, took communion, then hurried home out of the weather, typically foul for this time of year, and spent the afternoon listening to a football match on BBC radio.

Monday morning the rain had eased but a strong southeast wind was trying to uproot the roadside poplar trees. Under other circumstances, Harry might have driven his tiny four-cylinder Hillman down to Avonmouth, found a secure spot in one of the transit sheds and left it there so that he'd have transport to his front door when he got home. But today, for some unknown reason, he decided to take the county bus to the Tramways Centre, Bristol, and get a taxi from there to the Avonmouth, seven miles away.

"Keep warm, Harry. I know you get angry when I'm on at you all the time about keeping warm, but promise me you will." They kissed, just as they had always done, even in sterner times, and he was gone -- clutching a well worn leather suitcase. That was the last time Grace Dunning saw her husband.

*

Harry Dunning sat at a window seat watching the green, sodden farmland pass by, and thought of his retirement ten years from now; of his luck throughout the Battle of the Atlantic, which he'd survived unscathed, and of the upcoming trip. He knew little or nothing about frozen meat. Why, he wondered, they hadn't they picked a Houlder Bros. ship? They carry frozen meat from Argentina all the time. Oh, well, he thought.

*

Captain Dunning was on board by three o'clock in the afternoon. As he walked down the quay toward the gangway, he noted with some alarm that the forward draft of the vessel that towered above him, was a mere twelve feet, and wondered how she would behave at sea.

Stopping outside the mate's cabin on the way to his own, he made himself known to the chief officer by going straight to the point. "Mister Evans, is all the ballast in?

The mate nervously picked up a small grubby notebook off his desk and opened it. "Yes, sir, I haven't had the saltwater ballast tanks pressed up yet, but I will just as soon as we get clear of the lock gates."

"What about the fore peak?"

"That's fresh water, sir." The mate consulted the carpenter's grubby sounding book. "It's full, sir."

"What's the after draft?" Dunning asked with some anxiety in his tone.

"Fifteen foot-six", the mate replied. With a short grunt, Captain Dunning climbed the next set of steps to his room. While changing into his uniform, he thought about the ballast condition of his ship and began to focus on the forthcoming voyage. This was no trip to

Jamaica; this was a voyage into the birthplace of some of the world's worst storms.

With the aid of two tugs and a regular Bristol dock pilot, *Empire Abbey* was pushed and pulled down to the knuckle at the east end of the dock and carefully shoved into the lock. With still two hours to go until high water, Dunning took his ship past the Flatholm into the River Severn and westward toward the south coast of Ireland and the uninhibited wastes of the Atlantic.

At the end of WWII, merchant ships generally had no sophisticated navigation equipment such as Decca Navigator, Loran or Radar. They still relied on the antiquated magnetic compass and a sextant by which to fix the ship's position each day. There was a Radio Direction Finder (RDF) but this method of obtaining a single position line was unreliable, even under the best circumstances.

After passing the Fastnet, *Abbey* began to feel the full power of the ocean; long swells and a more aggressive sea. For the next twenty-four hours, she maintained a course of west-by-north, the first leg of a great circle which would, by making daily course adjustments, hopefully take her to a point some thirty miles south-by-east of Cape Race, Newfoundland.

By midnight when the third mate was about to go off watch, he noted that the barometer had begun to fall sharply, and that the wind had fallen away leaving an uneasy, threatening ocean. A brief break in the low stratus cloud revealed a few brilliant stars, friendly in their presence but soon obscured as the wind piped up from the north and strengthened to storm force.

"Barometer's falling, sir," said the third mate to the captain, who had spent the best part of the evening watch traveling from his cabin to the bridge, and back again.

"Thank you, Mr. Wright. Is the second mate there?"

"He's checking the ship's position in the chart room, sir. I'll let him know you're on the bridge."

Captain Dunning went into the chartroom.. "Good morning, Mr. Evans, although I must say I might wish for a better one than this. I wrote no night orders because I shall be on my day bed until this weather subsides. All you have to do is blow down the speaking tube and I'll be here. Just use your common sense and call me if you see anything unusual or become undecided about making a course change."

"Yes sir, I'll let you know if anything happens. Would you like a cuppa when you wake up?" Captain Dunning smiled and said, "That'd be nice."

The following morning the weather had not changed, except perhaps that wind had backed to a little west of north. *Abbey*, in her light condition, reacted to every swell that powered along from the northwest; panting as she became suspended across a roller that lifted her forefront high out of the water; pounding as the forefront returned to the ocean and smacked down onto the concrete-like surface with a bone-jarring thud that shook the ship as though it were in the grasp of a sea monster. Every longitudinal girder vibrated.

Whether on or off watch, getting comfortable under these violent conditions was an individual feat of ingenuity. The cook had much to worry about. Responsible for producing three hot meals a day for forty men, he first had to make sure that the oil galley fires were safely contained and that there were no leaks. He was cooking on top of a steel stove where the angular variation of the surface changed forty-five degrees every few minutes. Even though each pot and pan on the stove-top was held in place by steel fiddles (brackets), the pans themselves would often tilt to such a degree that the contents would spill.

During the most violent motion, the officer of the watch found himself a niche between two uprights and wedged himself in as comfortably and securely as possible. Moving from one place to another was restricted to the one-to two-minute lulls in the weather, when it was possible for him to dash into the chartroom and relieve himself or refill his cup of tea or coffee.

Captain Dunning had found himself a safe place seated on the pilot chair in the wheelhouse. His most comfortable pose was slouched against the bridge front next to the clear-view screen (A rapidly rotating glass disc) with one elbow on the window sill and the other arm stretched out clutching a cup of cocoa. A gyro compass connected to an auto-gyro pilot attempted to keep the ship on course. Whirling around frantically, it seemed to have a desire to escape from its gimbals.

Dunning phoned his owners on Wednesday, January 19 with the dismal news that the weather showed no signs of letting up and that they had covered a mere five hundred and seventy-five miles since passing the Fastnet – two thousand very nasty miles lay ahead.

"I might add," said Dunning to his owners with mock solemnity, "we are, to all intents and purposes, lost! We haven't seen the sky since we left. No sights! We'll get there in the end."

For the next seven days the mountainous sea raged and the swells rolled eastward with unrelenting power. In the minds of all those sailors, each day that passed was always "the last day of this lousy weather," but it never was. No sooner had the wind subsided to a mere force seven (forty-five to fifty knots), than it backed toward the southeast, bringing sleet and heavy rain squalls before freshening and veering toward the west and reaching storm force again.

The physical effects on the crew of being constantly on the move, going from one leg to another, trying to do their jobs under impossible conditions, exhausted them. They slept little, and the mental effect was one of depression.

*Abbey*, just two years old, showed that British shipbuilding was still the finest in the world. She was being subjected to the worst that the North Atlantic could throw at her.

With wearisome ruthlessness, the westerly-to-north-westerly storms continued unabated. This *Complex Low Pressure System,* as the meteorologists called it, was the result of the remains of a late tropical storm combining with a depression forming in the Davis Strait, between the coast of Labrador and the west coast of Greenland. (Anyone who has seen the movie *The Perfect Storm* will have witnessed this meteorological phenomenon).

Harry Dunning had been through storms before, many of them; he had also spent five years at sea as a defenseless target for the U-boat, but the present weather condition and all their attendant setbacks were taking their collective tolls on his usual placid disposition. The responsibility of being master had become second nature to him, but when faced with an uncontrollable exterior force that had denied him full command of his vessel, the strain and tension, not to mention lack of sleep, magnified the fear that had crept into his consciousness. The sum of all his fears would be the loss of his crew and the ship. He asked himself the same question a hundred times a day. Was this wartime vessel strongly enough constructed to withstand more of what she had already endured without breaking up? He had himself been down to the weather deck to examine the expansion joints on the bulwark rail, and found shiny steel where the pounding had bent the ship longitudinally like a steel girder. Logically, the joints were doing their job, but the realization that he could actually see evidence of the impact was unnerving. He was also worried about the propeller racing each time it left the ocean.

The captain had spoken to the chief engineer recently about the possibility of reducing the revolutions before the propeller left the water. He also explained that he needed to keep steerage-way by keeping the propeller turning at a certain number of revolutions.

The chief engineer nodded his head. "I'll see what I can do," he had said over his shoulder.

Allowing for set and drift, Captain Dunning figured that his ship was about fifty miles east of his original dead reckoning position. They still had close to one thousand miles to go.

At 8 am on January 21, the wind once again backed to the southwest and freshened to a full gale. In no time, the prospect of *hell afloat* turned into reality. Staggering ten feet without being hurled against a bulkhead or through a doorway you had just reached, became all too-vivid a reality. From lurching along at seven knots, *Abbey*, like a wounded beast which knows that the end is near, panted, groaned and floundered along in a stricken manner. The crew began to sense that this was an uneven contest that the ship would not win.

Captain Harry Dunning had not been feeling well for the past several days. Apart from being exhausted through lack of proper sleep, a deepening anxiety about the safety of his ship and crew seemed to have affected his judgment. Part of him knew that he should simply go below and rest for twelve hours; he might even get some sound sleep. Another part, his conscience, told him that if he put himself ahead of doing his duty as master (staying on the bridge, in command) he would be abandoning his duty to the crew. He vacillated between the two, and finally decided that when the next lull in the storm arrived, he would go below and rest. It was not to be.

Less than twelve hours after the wind had lost some of its force, a rogue sea whose crest towered forty feet above the *Abbey*'s bridge, swept the ship aside disdainfully and threw her twenty degrees off course.

"Hard a'starboard," gulped Dunning, having been nearly thrown out of his chair. "Bring her up into the wind."

The swell rolled relentlessly beneath *Abbey* and in doing so lifted her stern high out of the water. At 01.30 am on January 31, the drive shaft sheared at the bare end, hurling the propeller, their only sure means of survival, a thousand fathoms deep into the angry wastes of the Atlantic Ocean.

After a frantic shudder, the ships' main propulsion stopped; she became silent. All that could be heard was the roar of the storm and the seething hiss of the foam.

"We've lost the propeller, Captain." The chief engineer's anticlimactic announcement by engine-room-to-bridge telephone was followed by laconic acceptance.

"I know, Chief," said the captain. "Is everything okay down there?"

"Oh, I expect there'll be a few bearings busted; nothing to worry about – not yet, anyway."

"Come up and see me Chief, when you have a chance. We are in a perilous predicament." The chief engineer acknowledged the seriousness of the situation and said he'd be up directly.

During this brief exchange, the ocean wasted no time in taking charge. Without any driving power, *Abbey* had come up into the wind and wavered uncertainly poised atop a breaker whose genesis had probably been two hours earlier and seventy miles to the west. Catching the hapless ship on the starboard bow, the wave swung her violently farther to starboard and swept her down into the deep trough between swells where she broached, rolling violently putting the lee bulwarks underwater. Many of the crew were further injured, including the captain who bruised his right arm.

Painfully getting to his feet, Captain Dunning barked at the second mate, "Get the other mates up here right away, and tell Sparks to bring his pad in here."

Sparks was there first. "Get this out to Halifax Naval Control and send it C.Q. (to all ships):

*"Empire Abbey WE HAVE LOST OUR PROPELLER IN*
*DR. POSITION LAT: 48°50".N 47°50" W.*

*WEATHER: W.S.W FORCE 9. REQUIRE IMMEDIATE*
*ASSISTANCE.*
*Dunning —Master*

None of the officers, indeed none of the crew, had before experienced such a misadventure as this. From the expression on their faces, however, they all knew the possible consequences should assistance not arrive soon.

Captain Dunning's thoughts were running wild. There was no immediate solution to the problem; keeping the ship afloat until assistance arrived was his pressing concern.

"A sea anchor is what we need, Mr. Jones." He had addressed the mate but his appeal was to all three deck officers. "What do we have that will fill the bill? She's broached to at the moment. I fear for the safety of those lifeboats."

The mate echoed their collective solution. "The only suitable, accessible piece of equipment that comes immediately to mind is the Board of Trade gangway. What do you think, Captain?" The mate looked for approval. Everyone nodded.

"Have a care, Mr. Jones. Make sure that everyone on the weather deck has a lifeline on. Take the purchase from the heavy lift derrick, lead it aft and make it fast to the gangway at the platform end. I'll tell the chief to put power on the foredeck winches." Leaving the mate to make all this happen, Captain Dunning staggered back to the bridge.

It took the three mates and two able-bodied seamen two hours to release the wire from the heavy lift winch, manhandle the bare end through the bow chock lead (in the eyes of the ship) and lead it back to the gangway at No.3, hatchway where it was made fast to the steel structures of both the platform and the wooden gangway. Twenty minutes after that, the whole structure was released into the ocean. Slowly, agonizingly the ship was buffeted eastward leaving the newly created sea anchor to do its best to keep the ship's head into the wind and sea.

\*

*Franklin,* a steam salvage tug, recently returned from wartime activities in Europe to her home port of Halifax, Nova Scotia, lay quietly alongside. On board was a full stand-by crew, including her master, Harry Brushette, and chief engineer, Frank Poirier.

At 02 a.m on January 31, Sparks banged on Brushette's door. "SOS for you, Skipper; disabled cargo ship, *Empire Abbey.*"

"Okay, Sparks. Wake everyone up. We'll be sailing about 05.00. Keep your ear out for further signals from *Empire Abbey*. Thanks."

*Franklin* shifted to the oil dock; while she bunkered, a ship's chandler brought down fresh provisions to last ten days. Brushette's instincts told him that this rescue would require all the tricks of the trade and his salvage expertise. Of the *Franklin* herself, he had every confidence, especially so since his old shipmate, Frank Poirier, was chief engineer, a man who was able to coax the last bit of energy out of a steam engine that was constructed in a time when they knew how to build them. They had sailed together for many years and had accomplished many salvage rescues, some of them spectacular.

Two hours before dawn, *Franklin* slipped quietly out of Halifax harbor and headed in a general east-north-easterly direction toward Sable Island - and the fury of the mortal storm.

Captain Brushette, from his experience going to the assistance of vessels in distress, knew sailors' minds and shipmasters' stresses. He knew how all those men were relying on him and his salvage ship. This was by no means the first time he had proceeded into the vortex of two converging storms. His intuition told him that a light ship of *Abbey's* size without a propeller would probably be much more heavily influenced by the wind and sea than she would be when loaded.

Leaning against the chartroom table, a chart of the western portion of the North Atlantic Ocean spread out in front of him, Brushette turned over in his mind the mercurial behavior of an ocean he knew well.

"Well, Mr. Gandy," he said to his first mate, "I am going to stick my neck out and guess that she's somewhere close to . . .". He reached out and drew a small circle on the chart – "here." He measured the distance left to go and called the radio operator to send the following message to *Abbey.*

> *We will close with you about 11 p.m. at that time*
> *please fire a red rocket and repeat on demand.*

A few minutes after eleven, Franklin's lookout reported seeing a rocket close on the port bow. An hour later, she was lying alongside preparing the towing hawser for the long tow back.

*

At breakfast time on January 3, Captain Dunning sat in what had become known as *the Cap'ns spot* in the wheelhouse. He had eaten sparsely, but had consumed many cups of coffee and cocoa. He was not a well man. He had noticed that apart from becoming physically weaker, his brain wasn't functioning alertly and his eye sockets seemed to be drying out.

"Sir," said the third mate, lightly shaking his shoulder, "tug *Franklin* says she'll be here at eleven tonight," and handed him a message flimsy. Without a word the captain took the message and looked at it dazedly.

"At eleven, y'say? Ask the mate if he's ready for her, will you please?"

"Aye, sir," the junior officer replied. As an afterthought, he said, "Maybe you'd like to try and take forty-winks. Do you the world of good, sir."

"No thank you, Mr. Wright. I'm perfectly happy where I am. I've been here more than a week already; may as well sit the rest of the voyage out."

With all the deck arc-lamps blazing, and the two, *not-under-command* red lights hanging from the signal yard, *Abbey*, surrounded by a bright nimbus, looked like an encapsulated, snowy Christmas ornament.

"Break out the distress rocket box, third mate. If nothing else, it'll tell them we are paying attention.

About 11 p.m, the carpenter fired a distress rocket and the whole crew sent a faint but welcoming cheer a few minutes later at the sight of the brightly-lit *Franklin* as she appeared from behind a mountainous sea. Captain Dunning struggled to his feet and told the mate to take four men forward to receive the messenger line and the tug's towing hawser.

"For God's sake, be careful," he said, "I'll not be able to do a thing for you if you go over the wall."

Eager hands grabbed *Franklin's* messenger line as it rocketed over the forecastle head, and desperate men took it to the winch and hauled the heavy wire through the bow chock Panama lead.

Hauling off to the west-south-west, Brushette began the long, difficult tow of the crippled ship. Watching every lurch and pitch of both vessels, the salvage skipper nursed his charge along taking full advantage of every brief lull in the storm.

Both masters knew that it was merely a matter of time before the towing hawser would part, and the grave danger of losing both ships. Brushette had asked Dunning to see what he could do about securing *Abbey's* anchor in place and shackling the bare end of the anchor chain to the towing hawser — a tricky maneuver even in fair weather. *Abbey's* master declined; he considered it too dangerous.

Twice the hawser had parted, and twice, under the most punishing conditions Brushette had shown his worth by coming up under the lee bow of *Abbey* and unerringly placing the messenger across the foredeck. So close was he that he could see the haggard, desperate faces of the crew as they gazed expectantly at their champion. On the second occasion, *Abbey's* crew had hung the port anchor off and made the towing hawser fast to the chain. Once accomplished, and twenty-five fathoms of chain paid out of the chain locker, *Franklin* settled comfortably ahead of her charge steadied by the thirty tons of anchor chain.

During the previous forty-eight hours, both ships had drifted one hundred miles east; by the morning of January 8, that distance had been made up. Sable Island, a huge, barren offshore sandbank, appeared on their starboard beam at noon the following day; *Abbey's* first landfall in twenty-five days. The ocean, however, with a pent-up rage of its own, still seemed determined to end this voyage before its time.

Without pause, the storm backed to the southwest and increased in violence. Battered but steadfast with a sleepless Brushette in charge, *Franklin* struggled westward through the longest and most formidable North Atlantic weather patterns on record. Both crews and the ships they manned had just about reached the peaks of their endurance when, close to midnight on January 10, Marryat, *Franklin's* radio man, handed Brushette a message from *Abbey:*

*Our captain has just died. He had not slept for thirteen days.*

Completely unprepared for this piece of news, Brushette stood in the heaving wheelhouse contemplating this undeserved conclusion to an heroic human when he realized that the noise had abated. He opened the wheelhouse door and stepped onto the wing of the bridge.

The wind had died to a whisper.

All that was left was the angry hiss of the white foam as it surged by the bulwarks and distant muted crash of the sea's welter.

"I'll be damned," he muttered under his breath.

*

As the real fear of spending their last few minutes on earth in the frigid waters of the Atlantic faded, *Abbey's* crew tried to resume some kind of shipboard normalcy. Some slept, others ate. Captain Harry Cummings, however, had done neither. He didn't realize it, but life was slipping away.

"I can't rouse the captain. Go get the chief steward," the mate suggested. "See if he can rouse him."

At the beginning of the evening watch on Jan.10, the captain hadn't budged from his pilot's chair in the wheelhouse: hadn't even moved. He'd now been there for almost two weeks. Any efforts to urge him below, to sleep, had failed. He seemed to be semi-comatose.

Gripping him by both shoulders, the chief steward, Mr. Clarke, tried to slew him around, and then noticed the unusual pallor of the captain's face. A minute later, he blurted out, "Good God, he's dead."

A stunned silence settled over the mates gathered together in the wheelhouse. They looked at each other dumbfounded.

With a mixture of relief and sadness, the first mate stepped outside the wheelhouse and noted a change in the weather. The wind had died to a whimper. Far to the west in a dark blue clearing in the scud, a few stars winked brilliantly. Below the stars, where the horizon melded with an oily swell, the loom of the Sambro Light beckoned them in.

*Author's note: I thank Farley Mowat, author of "GREY SEAS UNDER," an account of numerous rescues by salvage tug "FRANKLIN" for his permission to extract pertinent details from his account of the rescue of EMPIRE ABBEY.*

*My brother Thomas Wright was third mate of EMPIRE ABBEY on this fateful voyage and witnessed all the main incidents on board. Much of the "atmosphere" on board he passed on to me before he died in Sydney, Australia in 1983.*

*PJW.*

\*

# Recovery from Alcoholism
*What shall we do with the drunken sailor?*

At a San Francisco halfway house, during one of my frequent shots at mastering the art of getting and staying sober, I rediscovered a poem by Francis Thompson called *The Hound of Heaven*. I had first seen it when I was four or five. It meant nothing to me then, but the brilliant morocco bookbinding caught my eye, and my mother's tears as she read it moved my young soul.

She told me she was crying because the poem was about a poor man looking for God. I can remember her hugging me at the time and rubbing her tear-stained face against mine and saying that He was with us at all times.

Growing up in an Irish Catholic family is no joke. There are rules for everything: bathing, going to the potty, going to bed, rules for what and when to eat, and they all seemed to have been instituted by God. And there was Sunday mass where you went to "visit" Him. But He wasn't there; He was inside a small white disc-like wafer. Very confusing. You had to believe a lot!

My father was a marine engineer and spent most of his time at sea. I hardly ever saw him. He never talked about God. He was killed in a maritime accident in 1937. My mother suffered greatly, but I didn't; I didn't know him.

With the small grant received from the steamship company, my mother, determined that she and the rest of the family might surely be granted easy entrance into heaven, sent me to a Dominican boarding school with the hopes that I would become their celestial passport. During the seven years I spent at that school, one of the priests made some nasty moves on me which curdled any positive thoughts I may have had about God – and the priesthood. I chose instead to go to sea like my Dad, my uncles and my granddad, all of whom happened to be alcoholic sailors.

For the young midshipman, life at sea was no picnic. Hard work seven days a week, twelve hours each day. We were allowed to go ashore at the discretion of the first mate.

At the age of seventeen I gave neither alcohol nor women a thought. Even though I had taken a swig from a bottle of sacristy altar wine when I was sixteen and become slightly tiddly I didn't consider it more than a silly joke. I doubt that had it tweaked my genes, it would have had the slightest effect on my future life. Time alone would tell.

One night while at anchor off the port of Boma, eighty miles up the Congo River, I was handed a gourd filled with *tombo,* native gin distilled from coconut. I overcame the appalling smell and discovered that two or three gulps transformed me from a shy, retiring boy into a real sailor. Two days later, after getting very drunk at *L'Hotel Metropole* in Matadi eighty miles upriver, the captain warned me of the perils of alcohol and threatened to cancel my indentures. Fear alone quenched the fires, but the damage had been done; the gene connection had been made. My future had been mapped.

I remained at sea for twenty-three years, passing examinations, and became captain during the last three. Somewhere between that first exciting drink in the Belgian Congo and my last desperate gulp in a desolate apartment in Portland, Oregon. I had crossed the line from social, to alcoholic, to addictive drinking, The final transition went unnoticed by me but not by those around me. "Go to A.A." they urged, I replied, "Those meetings are for alcoholics." And I firmly believed that my bizarre behavior would all go away if I could get my marriage straightened out, and my boss would only recognize what a valuable person I was.

I deserted my wife and five children in England in 1965, and came to the United States to live with another woman. I lied to both women and rationalized my atrocity. Now I had to feed my guilt as well as my disease. My alcohol intake increased, my work and family suffered, and I began to come apart.

My days started at 4.am with a Johnny Walker. At 6.a.m. another drink got me to work. I had a bottle in my desk. Lunch went from 11.30 until 1.30, and at 4 p.m. I decided to go home early. During these shiftless days, aware only of a deep seated anxiety, I failed to see the storm clouds gathering.

My wife dared to suggest that I had the makings of an alcoholic! This upset me greatly, but I nonetheless agreed to spend twenty-eight days in a recovery program. This was the first time I had attended a meetings of Alcoholics Anonymous, one of which was held in a pub not far from the recovery house. Those meetings! How inane they were. They kept on telling me to "Keep coming back" to do "*First things first*" and to "take it a day at a time." Then I figured it out. These programs were for "nice" people, like me, who drank too much. They certainly were not for the *alcoholic – the real alcoholic--* they couldn't afford it.

Relieved to know that all I had to do was control my drinking, I came home a new man, but there was something about those AA meetings that had ruined my drinking. The year was 1970. It would be another thirteen years before I took my last drink..

During my first week out I went to an A.A meeting downtown; it scared me. These people were *really* alcoholic. They looked terrible, they smelled terrible, and they were vulgar! I knew *these guys* shouldn't drink. This was not the place for an intellectual person like me. Six weeks later I had started drinking again. It was as though I had never stopped. I knew nothing about the silent progression of the disease. I knew nothing about me. I knew nothing about the disease and I was unwilling to learn. Like a sailor without a compass on a ship without a rudder, I was heading for shoal water.

One afternoon, shortly after a protracted luncheon, I was summoned to the director's office and fired. After the initial shock of realizing that I was out of a job, it dawned on me that perhaps this was supposed to happen, and that my problems would probably go away now that I was free of all that stress. I also knew that if I were to get another job, I'd better not go for an interview with alcohol on my breath. I stopped drinking and eventually started my own marine investigation business. My wife was happy, as were my friends and neighbors who all welcomed me back into society. The business flourished, and for nine months I showed all the outward signs of a new life. I did not know however, and neither did my friends and neighbors, that I wasn't just a heavy drinker who had stopped drinking, but that I was a mentally diseased mortal who had not dealt with my illness. My disease was only dormant.

In each of us, in all our walks of life, male and female, there is a part of the brain that figures things out; if it's going to rain, take an umbrella; if we are going out to eat, take some money; if it's a sunny day, let's take our swim suits and go to the beach, and so on. Although I didn't know it at the time, my mind worked differently; I had the mind of an alcoholic: it works like this. If it's going to rain, don't bother to go outside because it'll be miserable, so stay at home and have a drink. If we are going out for a meal, let's get there early so that can have a couple of drinks first. On sunny days I might have gone to the beach, but with a couple of six-packs. Drinking alcohol becomes the primary goal of every activity.

Whether I am consciously thinking about drinking or not, I have a hidden obsession that acts like a lodestone or the north-seeking end of a compass needle – I am genetically and physiologically attracted to, and obsessed with alcohol. I have a *justification committee* in my frontal lobe which becomes very active when I am not drinking. The first step on its agenda is to remind me that I don't have a problem with alcohol; I have a problem with other people in my life. If only they would try to understand me, I'd be a much better chap.

After nine months of enormous success with my business, new car, new house, I was leaving a small riverfront town one evening and my committee decided that life was so wonderful it was time to celebrate. I stopped and had a few glasses of wine - wine was okay! A week later I was feeling irritable and had more to drink. A week after that, it happened that my contract with a main principal was cancelled. My business folded and I decided that the booze would hold me together. I also began to suspect that I had a problem.

For two years I went from job to job, specialized investigation using my maritime expertise. One group sent me to North Africa, to Algeria and Egypt. "Go easy on the booze, Peter. If you get drunk in any of those Arab countries, they'll put you in jail and forget you." My committee had no solution for that problem. Dryer than the Sahara, more brittle than the pyramids, I fled from Egypt and started drinking again on a plane to Greece.

In spite of the drawbacks, as I called them, I considered my life under control. I had a job, a wife and two children who loved me. . . ( I never thought of the wife and kids I'd left in England), an expense account – and a swanky MGB drop head. But I was sorely afraid.

My next and last employer sent me to Fiji to inaugurate a new service. I had been dry for three or four weeks. I fell in with an old shipmate on Suva and arrived back in San Francisco two days late, barely remembering the events of the last week. My wife refused me entry into the house; my friends no longer knew me.

I was running now, but footsteps were close behind. I had no plans; I hardly had a working brain. Two former friends in the City took me down to the detox on Howard Street and asked the counselor to take care of me. Then without a drink for several hours, I walked out and found a few of San Francisco's forgotten who gave me some of their Thunderbird.

I spent that night crouched beneath the freeway feeling no physical pain. Fragments of my life paraded through my mind like mummers, taunting, reproaching, daring me to end it all.

The following morning, a remnant of reason led me back to the detox and eventually into a halfway house in the city. It was in this humble sanctuary that I learned that love was not something that only happened between the sheets, that caring was not dropping a coin in an alms box, and that true honesty would get me everywhere. I found some friends and did my best to settle in. Meetings of Alcoholics Anonymous became a regular feature. The concept of the Fellowship appealed to me – one drunk helping another, but the *how it works* part didn't appeal to any of my senses. I understood who or what they meant by a Higher Power, but the God I knew, or thought I knew at the time, was far too clinical, too ethereal to be of much use other than to adore, as I had been taught by my mother and by the priests at school.

The closest person to me during my stay at that halfway house was the house manager, Rusty. She told me her story – and taught me honesty. She was simple and straightforward, traits I envied. One hot afternoon in the city, she offered me some old books.

"Here Peter, some of these are written by countrymen of yours. There's one in particular I think you'd like." It was Francis Thompson's

*The Hound of Heaven."* I took it to my room and started reading those poignant lines:

> *I fled Him down the nights and down the Days;*
> *I fled Him down the arches of the Years;*
> *I fled Him down the labyrinthine ways*
> *Of my own mind, and in the midst of tears, I hid from Him."*

Francis Thompson.1859-1907.The Hound of Heaven

I remembered my mother's tears . . . and I began to understand.

The more I read of Thompson's epic, the more I identified with him as a man, and with his fear.

Francis Thompson, born into a devout Catholic family at the end of the 19th century was sent to Upshaw College in the North of England, where his father, a doctor, hoped that young Francis would become a priest. The principals at Upshaw thought differently and sent him home. Francis tried writing poetry but failed to make a living. During his literary forays he took opium to heighten his senses, as many writers were accustomed to doing, and got hopelessly addicted. At the turn of that century, realizing that he needed more than human help to survive, or indeed to remain sane, he turned to his Higher Power – and listened to what his struggling mind had to say. Thus was born his epic poem.

And thus I was able to combine the present results of my own predicament with Rusty's honesty, Thompson's cry for help, and the daily messages I heard from Alcoholics Anonymous ; it was the sound of a distant trumpet, an awakening.

Almost a year had passed at the halfway house, and I thought I had become well. I was about to learn, however, that although certain features of my makeup had changed, I had not accepted myself for who I really was a chronic, arrogant drunk still afflicted with a serious disease.

Just before Christmas, I had an offer of work on the Columbia River in Portland.Oregon. Without giving future consequences a thought, I took the offer and told Rusty. How could I have refused? My *committee* had already decided that it was time for me to move along. "This is your chance Peter. They know you're a good man. They have plans for you up there in Oregon. Just think: you've beaten the drinking problem and you are going to show them what you can really do when you are sober." Rusty's last tearful words were, "You know where to find us."

That winter in Portland was the coldest on record. The Columbia froze over and navigation on the river was restricted to daylight transits. My work was cut in half. I had more time on my hands that I anticipated. Nonetheless, January went by in a flurry of busy learning. I worked from dawn to dusk and retired to my tiny apartment each evening as contented as my unhealed mind would allow me. But I was lonely, and AA meetings just didn't do it for me. My attempts to make friends with women were unsuccessful – and Francis Thompson was drowned out by my "committee's" raucous arguments.

Depressed and feeling isolated, I drove out of Portland one morning bound for Everett, where I had two ships to attend. Half way down the river road, my water pump blew. Coasting to a nearby exit, I braked and skidded down the off-ramp and stopped directly outside a large flashing neon sign – BUDWEISER! My "committee" notified me that this was a sign. The bartender told me where the nearest mechanic worked, and I spent the next two hours telling my life story over a few scotch and sodas.

Why? Why had I once again taken a drink? It was surely a true measure of my insanity. Maybe this time it would be different. And for the following five days, it was. I continued to work but I had to stop several times on the highway to stop myself from shaking too much. I never left home without a bottle.

The *Big Book* tells us of *incomprehensible demoralization*. I had read it, but paid little heed to it. Now, ten days after I had rekindled my disease, I had another of my *All Souls* experiences, when my past, both real and unreal, came back to haunt me with their hideous laughter and accusatory pointing fingers. Neither wine nor liquor eased my searing mind. I fled – back to San Francisco where I hoped that friends would once again rescue me. They did, for the last time.

Another treatment program! Would I ever get the knack of living sober? What did I lack? What was I missing? One of the counselors told me during a specially arranged interview.

"It's a long time since I met anyone like you, Peter. You are reasonably bright, but you lack the milk of humanity. You are a selfish snob. You are the only person in your life." He went on for half an hour; never said anything nice about me. It hurt . . . but it worked.

It was on Steiner Street, in a magnificent-old-mansion-turned-halfway-house, that I finally fused Francis Thompson's humility with the simplicity of the suggestions of Alcoholic Anonymous. And I paid attention to the straightforwardness of my fellow alcoholics, their willingness to go to all lengths to attain and maintain sobriety.

In one of Thompson's desperate moments he hears his God caution him: "All Things betray thee who betray Me." I still do not understand some of Thompson's rhetoric but I know that he was baring his soul, revealing his own inner turmoil and lack of perception. He, in his hours of desperation, like me in mine, was pleading for help. I joined this unhappy man in our quest for peace.

Including my Maker, I had betrayed my family, friends and all who had trusted me. In Step Three of the Twelve Steps of Alcoholics Anonymous, It is suggested that we turn our will and our lives over to the care of God, as we understood Him. I had, in fact, never once taken the suggestions contained in the Twelve Steps seriously.

I would like to share some of the poignant expressions of anguish that came from Thompson's soul, which so clearly describe our plight and which helped me recognize a *Power greater than myself.*

*"Naught shelters thee, who will not shelter Me."*

\*

*"My mangled youth lies dead beneath the heap, my days*
*Have crackled and gone up in smoke.*

\*

*"And why should anyone set you apart to love?*
*Human love needs human merits!*
*And how have you merited, dingiest of men?*
*Alas, you don't know how unworthy you are.*
*Who will you find to love, ignoble thee?*
*Save Me, save only Me."*

This week, I am sober twenty-three years, and for that gift I have immeasurable gratitude toward the Fellowship and to my Maker for giving me the courage to stay the course and embrace humility. I also acknowledge with some wonder, the synchronous events that linked my first encounter with "The Hound of Heaven" with the last, in my time of need.

*Redding, California*
*January 27, 2006*

\*\*\*

# Blessed are the Meek

## *"Half the Proper Sailor's Work is done upon his knees"*

After I got sober, I periodically had startling dreams of being naked on Market Street in San Francisco. There was little variation in the set and setting of each dream. I would be standing naked in a shop doorway, waiting for a streetcar and very conscious of my nudity while desperately covering my privates with cupped hands. In the dream I felt uncomfortable, but not sufficiently so as to make me run for cover. I always got on the tram and stood strap-hanging conscious of being stared at. No one said anything; they simply condemned me with their hostile looks. The dream always ended before the ride was over and I would wake sweating, trying to catch my breath. I wondered and worried about these dreams. What did they mean? Was I a pervert? I told my alcohol counselor about them and was told that they were quite normal for a person in my present mental state. He explained that they arose from feelings of insecurity and a sense of worthlessness. As the dreams continued, I found them less disturbing. Once or twice I found myself wondering how it would be for me if I ever actually found myself naked on Market Street – naked in public, on a tram! I was certain that it would be the most distressing, most disturbing thing that could ever happen to me.

I was wrong. That same year I would experience perhaps the most humiliating encounter of my life – on Market Street, San Francisco.

\*

In 1978, bad behavior got me into deep trouble with my wife, who eventually asked me to leave the house. The law occasionally escorted me to jail. My employers fired me. Alcohol and its unhappy and out-of-control captive were responsible for all of the above. I spent one night under a freeway on-ramp in the city, thinking about life and death. I believe it was under that concrete tomb that I finally surrendered, inwardly agreeing that I was powerless over alcohol. Instead of walking into the south -bound traffic, I stumbled into the city detox. I had neither plan nor ambition, but the counselors at that detox had come for me. They arranged for me to enter a half-way house in the city. They saved my life.

The half-way house, a lovely old mansion on Steiner, had retained much of its stateliness, albeit now occupied by twenty recovering alcoholic men from all walks of life. The rules of the house were simple: Stay sober, get a job, pay the rent, rejoin the human race.

The idea of getting a job appealed to me but the jobs on the board were not the type I was looking for. Something in the managerial field, I thought, not a swanky job but one where I could use my experience. No new jobs were posted the following day, and none the day after that.

"You'd better find a job, Peter, otherwise you'll be out of here week after next." The chief counselor knew all about "tough love."

I sulked a lot in those early days of sobriety. True thankfulness was an unknown quality. Gratitude began and ended with thanks a lot. When someone accused me of being arrogant, I became outraged, insulted, but that is exactly what my A.A sponsor told me when I presented him with my dilemma.

"How long have you been sober, Peter, a couple of months, eh?" I should have seen the storm clouds gathering.

I didn't think it necessary to answer him. Then he told me that I was "an arrogant conceited prick". " It really hurt, but somewhere the bell of truth rang.

I called the number under *casual labor*, and made an appointment to see someone called Richard at eight the following morning.

I love San Francisco, especially so on a clear day such as the one on which I boarded the trolley to start my first day as a laborer! Even though the trolley was packed I had time to ruminate. It had dawned on me that the guys I was living with were far better adapted to living a day-by-day existence. They were tougher than I, better at surviving than I. I thought of my sponsor's condemnation and knew it to be true – almost! I was a long way from being honest with myself. Life had been too easy for me. There had always been someone there to rescue me; someone to whom I could flee for shelter.

I got off at Post and Market and walked one block back to Sutter. It was seven-thirty. The forgotten souls of that city were hunched up against lampposts or crouched in doorways wrapped in newspapers to keep themselves warm. I wanted to ignore them but – *wasn't I one of them just a few weeks ago?* The reality of my present social standing had begun to impinge on my arrogance. I didn't like it. I was unable to take this part of my life as a new beginning, and not as a continuation of the one I'd left behind when I entered the halfway house.

Even as I stood outside this dilapidated, six-story building on Sutter, I suffered a few misgivings and very nearly turned away. Dumpsters on the sidewalk contained debris from the upper rooms of what used to be an infamous rooming house. The canopy over the two front glass swing-doors was torn, the uprights bent. A thousand pieces of discarded chewing gum added to the general air of dinginess and decay. Through the glass front door I could see some activity and was somewhat reassured to find an air of elegance in a spacious lobby. A few potted palms were positioned at the foot of what was once a regal stairway, and a lighted chandelier hung over an expensive carpet.

Near the elevators I could see a group of individuals gathered around a man dressed in a business suit. As I approached, one of the listeners caught the speaker's attention and pointed at me. The speaker pirouetted on his dais, gave me a glare then turned his back on me and went on talking.

"Excuse me, I'm looking for Richard." The pirouetter looked over his shoulder at me and said, "Wait a few minutes please," and went on talking. He seemed to be giving his crew orders for the day. I found a place by a potted palm and waited.

*

I had guessed that Richard was gay but not flamingly so, but friendly and warm. I took to him immediately. Pleased with myself for not running away, I agreed to start wallpapering those rooms stripped and ready; piece of cake really. Small rooms with no alcoves or walk-ins. I figured I could do two rooms in three days.

Later, after our friendship had developed, Richard, the manager of the hotel, told me that he had put his life saving's into remodeling this down-at-heel rooming house and scoured the Castro District for employees. Harvey Milk, a gay city supervisor was Richard's hero and supported the gay movement in San Francisco wherever possible. Milk became a political target and eventually the target of a deranged ex-cop who walked into the civic center one morning and shot the supervisor as he sat at his desk. The murderer was given a speedy trial and pled not guilty by way of insanity. The verdict showed that the ex-cop was indeed insane, because, they said, he ate too many "Twinkies" (a sugary doughnut-type bun) which had upset his sugar level and made him "hyper."

I worked four of the five working days. On Thursdays I attended a class on alcoholism at the U.C Outreach in the city. I thought that I would become a counselor. I did eventually succeed in passing Part B of the course, no great achievement but the time spent gave an insight into the physical and mental aspects and mores of the disease I walked around with.

Every day Richard and I made time to chat over a cup of coffee. He too was a recovering alcoholic. I learned from him that being gay and alcoholism went hand in hand. In those days being gay was predominantly socially unacceptable. Gays were often unable to get employment or were fired for being gay. Life was not made easy for them. Thirty years later, not much has changed in a society which still has a medieval, puritanical mentality.

We discussed our personal problems, how to adjust in a hypocritical society, the importance of A.A. and forming friendships. From him I learned a lot about myself, most of all the importance of being honest. Because I attended U.C Berkeley each Thursday, he dubbed me the Student Prince.

By the end of spring, eight others had joined the workforce. Richard appointed me foreman – he paid me $9 an hour – a princely wage! By the end of summer, the hotel was nearing completion and I had laid off all but three workers.

"You know, Peter, we'll be opening soon and I have to ask you one more favor." Richard pulled me aside one morning and led me by the arm to the front lobby doors.

"Next week," he went on, "two of our gentlemen from England will be arriving and I really want the outside of the hotel cleaned up a bit." He pointed to the sidewalk. "What can you do about all those nasty blobs, you know, the chewing gum, stuck to the sidewalk?"

The request took me by surprise because of the immediate implications I envisioned: me on my hands and knees on the sidewalk . . . but how could I refuse? Richard knew the answer long before he'd asked the question.

We agreed upon the size of the area of the sidewalk to be cleaned up. I chalkmarked it out into six squares and we went to work at eight o'clock the following morning.

As I knelt down, scraper in hand, I wondered how I could make this singularly distasteful job more interesting. Why do Americans chew gum? Other nations who do not regard the United States with awe do not chew gum. Perhaps it is because they substitute that mandibular exercise with smoking. But so many chew and smoke at the same time. Does it help them to think? Do you suppose they think it makes them look tough , laid- back?

I attacked each blob of gum with a vengeance. The stuff that had been there for ages came off relatively easily, but the freshly expectorated pink latex stuck to the edge of the steel scraper and had to be removed with my forefinger and thumb. I had removed a dozen or so of the shameful disfigurements and was sitting back on my heels eyeing what was left, when I sensed that the nearby pedestrian traffic had been somehow interrupted. Someone was standing behind me. Before I could swivel and see who it was, a faintly familiar voice shattered my equilibrium.

"My God, is that you captain? Captain Wright, is that you?" I froze. The voice was that of an employee with whom I had worked for years before the agency had fired me. My worst nightmare had come to pass. I wished *The Big One* would open up the earth and swallow me.

Slowly I got to my knees, then one knee and straightened up, turned around and faced the beaming smile of Jimmy Steele. He extended a hand.

"Good God, man, I thought you were in Singapore or Hong Kong or someplace like that. What the hell are you doing on your knees on Market Street?"

I had no story to tell, no excuse; there was nothing I could think of to say that would pour balm on a raw, unexplainable situation. Then one of those miracles occurred; you know, one you hear of during the early days of your meetings at Alcoholics Anonymous.

"Peter! Oh, Peter!" Richard's voice overrode the midmorning racket of the central thoroughfare of the city. "You have an urgent telephone call. They say they can't wait."

I could see Richard's arm waving frantically from the front doors.

A wave of relief washed over me. A reprieve! Turning briefly to Jimmy Steele, I murmured something about *having to leave and seeing him sometime later,* and almost fell over myself rushing to the hotel entrance.

Richard grabbed my still-shaking arm and led me to the coffee shop.

"Thanks for that, Richard," I managed to blurt out. "You saved my life."

He looked compassionately at me for a minute or two. "You have so much to learn, Peter, so much basic stuff. Don't ever forget what A.A tells us: "Leave behind your old life and start a new one". Pride is part of your old life; leave it behind. I could see that you would certainly hurt yourself trying to explain, to lie to your friend out there. Scraping detritus off the sidewalk is a noble act! Getting on your hands and knees to do it is a sign of humility." He paused for a moment, then put his arm around my shoulders. "You have to let go of the idea that humility is a weakness. It is, in fact, moral fearlessness."

The hotel opened on time amid great rejoicing among the gay community. I had moved on, back into the steamship business, a move which proved disastrous for me, but Richard's words of wisdom stayed with me and stood me in good stead during those difficult times.

*

# The Liverpool Irish Fireman

## His Evolution and Disappearance

I was introduced to the Liverpool Irish fireman when I joined *Calumet* in Hull on March 3, 1944. I was seventeen. That day was memorable, not only because I came to know of a breed of man hitherto unknown to me, but because I had entered the tough, profane world of the Merchant Navy after seven years in the hallowed halls of a Dominican boarding school.

I signed on *Calumet,* a coal-fired steam turbine merchant ship of some 10,000 tons, a typical waterborne workhorse of the North Atlantic. A crew of sixty-three saw to it that she got where she was supposed to, and that she was properly maintained. The man- power which created the horsepower to drive the ship through the ocean at twelve knots was comprised of twenty-four firemen/trimmers, most of them Irish and all of whom seemed to live on Scotland Road or London Road, Liverpool when they were not at sea. Referred to, on board, as the *Black Gang,* these gentlemen, whose sole job was to slice coal into manageable lumps, haul it thirty feet from the coal bunker to the stoke hold and shovel it into the furnaces, earned the reputation of being the most incorrigible creatures God had ever made. If, for no apparent reason, a fight erupted, you could be certain that at the center of the fracas you would find a Liverpool fireman. Perhaps it was their confinement in the bowels of the ship aggravated by a backbreaking, boring job that caused them to be short-tempered, but I rather think that their attitude to society in general was that of rebellion borne of a hundred tales of hardship under British administration, handed down from generations of residents to generations of immigrants who never forgave Elizabeth I and James II for their callousness.

On board ship they kept very much to themselves although their general remarks could be heard by everyone within earshot. Most of the conversation was profane, inane, insulting banter, some of which may have been directed toward a junior engineer, who had undoubtedly been warned by a senior engineer to avoid contact with these strange creatures. Woe betides the young engineer who took umbrage and got into an argument; he might find his bunk filled with steam flies (nasty cockroaches which inhabited the galley) or a bucket of oily nuts and bolts.

They were a terror in Montreal, Halifax, Boston or New York, where forgiving police forces brought their live but useless bodies back to the foot of the gangway after a grand night in one of the many Irish bars that abound these East Coast ports. Unabashed and unrepentant, they resumed their duties in phlegmatic silence. But on the West African Coast their exuberance was confined to the forecastle where they lived. It wasn't the police herald who hauled them out of Joe Biff's on Sacrament Street that got the chief engineer's attention, but the silence of unconsciousness as most of the black gang lay stupefied after drinking African gin guaranteed to cause horrifying hallucinations.

The most interesting characteristic of the Liverpool Fireman was his exaggerated rolling gait, nicknamed a *Western Ocean Roll*, more noticeable, of course, after he had been ashore. Wearing oiled stoke-hold boots, blue serge pants held in place by a broad leather belt carefully arranged around his middle so that the buckle nestled comfortably six inches below his navel, allowing a nurtured obscene pot-belly to hang gravidly over the leather. He was quite the picture. Covering his oil stained singlet (chain breaker) he wore an ill-fitting, unbuttoned serge jacket. Rolling along as though the world belonged to him, both thumbs tucked into the front part of the belt, he strode, pigeon-toed, in an inadvertent, curiously seductive manner. He seemed to surge forward, propelled by the side-to-side undulation of his bottom. It was his way of displaying territorial invincibility in the face of foreign antagonism , imagined or real.

Oil-burning ships soon put an end to the reign of the fireman/ trimmer, but not before the Battle of the Atlantic and the U-boat gave so very many of those men a watery grave. Those on watch, and the engineers with them, didn't have a chance when a torpedo struck. Those men who sailed with my father, firemen Patini, Brown, Oliver and Meek, West Country men, all lost their lives when their vessel sank in the North Sea, my father too. I knew them well, rather they knew me, and passed on to me, a boy of ten, two gravely important messages: "Never judge a man by the color of his fingernails; death comes swiftly and unexpectedly to all of us".

I cannot say that the passing of the Liverpool fireman into archival legendary left an ache in my heart, neither do I suggest that they were the backbone of the Merchant Navy. I do, however, experience a certain nostalgia as I write this article. These men, the poor and deprived of Liverpool's throwaways, who went to sea and performed the most menial, backbreaking, dangerous work under the worst maritime conditions in order to feed their families, will forever have my respect.

\*

# The Greasy Palm

*"Money can't buy you love."*

*The Beatles*

When the telephone shattered the silence at 2:35 on a warm summer night in Southern California, my wife gave a resigned sigh, turned over and lay listening. I knew, and she too, that it could be nothing other than another maritime assignment.

Propping myself up on an elbow, I said, "Hello."

"Is that Captain Wright?"

An Englishman, I thought. It'll be a sensible job at any rate. "Speaking"

"Sorry to bother you at this time of day, but this job just came out of the blue from one of our Greek contacts. I wanted to get to you first to secure your services for our Club (Insurance Company) Newcastle United; hence the call at this ungodly hour. Not ungodly for us, but it is for you."

This was not an unusual occurrence. One's name gets around in London and suddenly one becomes a preferred investigator.

"That's okay," I said, quickly going through the jobs I had lined up for that day. "Tell me where the job is and when you want me to be there."

"It's in Ensenada, Mexico, and we'd like you to be there as soon as you can. It's a big job. By the way, my name is James McNabb and I represent new policies."

"Alright, James, I'll be there, but please put all details available to you on my printer as soon as you can. I may have some questions. I really don't feel like doing that right now."

"Will do," he said cheerfully, and hung up.

"Where to now?" The muffled query came like an arrow to my heart. I knew my wife didn't like me going away, and I'd spent far too much time abroad during the past couple of years to brush this job off as a "nothing job."

"It's a four or five hour drive to Mexico, a couple of days there. I should be home in three days." I gave her a squeeze and attempted to get a few more winks.

*

Instructions were on my printer when I arrived at the office a few hours later.

*GRYPHEN seven (7) hold geared bulk carrier. Loaded potash in Canada*

*4/5/81. Sailed for Bremen 4/6/81. Subsequent rough weather off California coast revealed ingress water into No.7 hold. Further examination revealed shell plating at No .6 and No .7 on the starboard side disconnected from approximately ten (10) frames.*

*Ship owner's abandoned the voyage and sought refuge at Cedros Island where charterer's eventually arranged for another vessel to take bulk potash using Gryphen's gear. Owners opted to put vessel into Ensenada for repairs and put her up for sale on the London Market. We have been approached by prospective buyers in Pireaus, Greece, Messrs. N. Tikkos, for coverage. Please meet Mr. Andropoulos on board for further owners' information, and submit complete condition report within one week. signed J McNabb.*

There was enough information in McNabb's report for me to determine that this would indeed be a two-day job. I confirmed receipt of Newcastle's message, included my rates and a day on which they could expect a preliminary report, told my assistant what jobs to take over, and set off for Mexico.

Even in those days, the U.S./Mexican boarder was like a circus, but an hour saw me through and an hour later I drove into Ensenada where I booked myself into a Holiday Inn.

*

I had been in Ensenada before on similar jobs. It was, to my mind, a twopenny-hapenny port of refuge, a place where the dollar went a long way, depending into whose pocket it went; labor was cheap and consequently rough and ready.

I decided to take a look at the ship but not start the survey at this late hour.

Gryphen lay in a floating dock at the only repair facility in Northern Mexico. A typical bulk carrier fitted with steel hatch covers and a 10-ton electric crane at each of the seven holds. One of the most depressing settings I know of is a vessel in drydock or undergoing repairs in a dockyard. The ship is dead and those working at the repairs have no interest in her, a bit like ship abuse.

From where I stood on the dockside, I could see the brilliant blue flicker of a welding rod on steel. Two plates from the sheer strake (the uppermost plates that are attached to the deck-plating had been removed and were lying on the dock. Half a dozen laborers were working off a wooden stage hanging against the ships' side. No way of telling how the repairs would take.

I climbed on board by way of a gangway that led up to the accommodation aft.

The usual litter lay in black plastic bags, some of it spilling out: beer bottles and cans, banana skins and orange peels. I inwardly tut-tutted and told myself that this was never the scene on my ships.

On my way to the captain's quarters I noted that the crew's quarters were empty and idly wondered how long that garbage had been lying there.

A curtain hung over the entrance to the captain's room, a practice that indicated that the master was either asleep or unavailable. The time was now 4:30. As I knocked on his door, I felt a little uneasy.

A shuffling and bumping told me that he had just gotten up. The door opened and the curtain was roughly pulled aside revealing a very un-captain-like individual. Pudgy, debilitated face, scrub-cut hair, pajama bottoms pulled up over a soiled Henley vest.

Two blood-shot eyes barely focused on my face. "Ja? What can I do for you?" he asked in a strong German accent.

Unwilling to talk ships with the man in this condition, I tried to postpone the interview. "Er . . . sorry captain; perhaps I should have phoned first. I'll come back tomorrow. My name is Peter Wright. I'm a surveyor representing a U.K. Club interested in insuring this ship."

"We knew you were coming. Come inside." He pulled the door back and at the same time indicated his own appearance with a deprecating wave of his hand. "Forgive my looks," he said, "had a rough night last night." He sought my understanding with a sly grin. "Scotch, Pepsi or coffee?"

"I'll not be here long," I hastened to let him know. "Nothing thanks. I'll just get some ship's particulars and try not to bother you until I've completed my survey."

The captain went into his bedroom and I noted all the ships details, her last survey and any deficiencies held over yet to be completed. The ship was classed Lloyds 100A1. This simply meant that the last time the ship had been subjected to a class survey, she had met all the requirements. I noticed that the date was not too long ago.

"Perhaps you would like to stay for dinner, Captain Wright?" The voice of the captain coincided with my completion of everything I needed to do. I declined as gracefully as I could. Before I left, I asked Captain Streiker if he would see to it that all the hatch covers be open upon my arrival at 7 am the following morning.

"They are completely empty, sir, and so far as I know, no damage has been reported anywhere else on the ship except at Nos. 6 and 7 shell plating."

"If I am going to complete a condition report for the Club, I must see everything," I explained, "so, if you please, have the hatch covers open." I could see that he was unhappy about this simple request and wondered why. "And ask Mr. Andropoulos, whom I understand is here from Greece, to be available sometime tomorrow. Thank you, Captain." He nodded assent, and I left the ship excited about spending the evening watching Mexican television.

As I stowed a camera, voice recorder and handy hammer into the numerous pockets of my boiler suit, I felt the interest mounting, as it always does when I'm about to start a condition survey. What maritime wonders will I discover today? Or, how could a ship sail around the oceans of the world in this condition?

After a cup of coffee with Captain Streiker I took a stroll around the weather deck. Everything looked just as I would expect it to look – nothing shipshape – nothing alive.

To make things look as though I actually worked for a living, I descended into No. 7 hold to view the progress of the replacement of the shell plating. Nothing exciting to be seen down there either. The workers were tack-welding the strake below sheer in place. That would eventually be Lloyd's surveyor's job.

This ship, I noted, had been fitted with a centerline duct-keel through which passed all the pipelines from the fore peak and the lower ballast tanks. The manhole covers were off. I decided, against my better personal judgment, but under pressure from my professional beliefs, to make a quick inspection of the relief valves. I tend to panic in very confined spaces and therefore avoid ballast tank inspections whenever possible. The tank was of standard depth – 36", but much of the interior space was occupied by two 8 inch ballast lines. Crouched on my hunkers I knelt down, ducked my head under the tank top plating and began to worm my way aft, trying to inspect the condition of the pipe and look out for butterfly valves. I finally reached the first one in line and found that it was seized up. Enough for me, I thought. I'm getting out of here. Trying to worm backwards was not so easy. My foot got jammed in something, and the first emotional quivers in my cerebral cortex began to signal a panic attack. DON'T PANIC, PETER, another part of my brain screamed. I heard it and simply lay still, aware of the shallowness of my breathing and the rapid pace of my heartbeat. THINK! THINK! I dislodged my foot at last and very slowly began to ease myself backwards down this long, very dark tunnel. I began to think of my Dad who had been drowned many years ago, and wondered if this kind of panic had been his last emotional experience.

With a great deal of comfort I saw the light getting brighter in my peripheral vision. Then I crawled up onto the tank top and breathed an enormous sigh of relief. Why did I bother to go into dark, dangerous places? I recorded my first observation of this condition survey.

Strolling over to the starboard side plating situated just forward of the damage under repair, I saw a deep fracture in the existing shell plating at tank top level. I thought they may or may not repair that but it will have to be doubled – as a temporary repair. As I worked my way forward through the remaining holds, I became aware of various minor damages which could be fixed one way or another, but from the tank top, looking up towards the underside of the weatherdeck and the plating of the upper wing ballast tanks, I could see some irregularities, the exact nature of which I could not determine from that distance.

I finally climbed out of No .1 hold, inspected the bow section then headed into the second half of the survey. The upper wing tanks at No. 1, as in the remaining holds, extend the length of the hold and are simply ballast tanks under the weatherdeck filled when necessary to reduce the metacentric height when the ship is rolling violently – to raise the center of gravity.

I could hardly believe my eyes. From inside the tank I had a clear view of the lower hold through numerous rusty holes from several inches to several feet in diameter. It was obvious that these water ballast tanks had not been used as such-- for a long time. A quick look at the condition of the remaining upper wing tanks revealed them to be in similar shape. I sat for a minute or two with my legs dangling through two holes into No. 6 hold thinking about the rest of the ship. Did the rest of the ship matter? Not as far as I was concerned. Each of the upper tanks would have to undergo major repair and the entire upper structure pressure testing. And I would be able to save the Insurance Club half of my fees.

At 12:30 I returned to the captain's room and found both him and Mr. Andropoulos finishing lunch. I introduced myself to the Greek representative.

Apparently high up in the hierarchy, maybe the owner's nephew, Andropoulos was a good looking young man in his thirties, well dressed and reeking of expensive cologne.

"Ah, Captain Wright, so soon, eh?" I sensed a certain nervousness in his query.

"Did either of you know about the condition of the upper wing tank plating?" I asked in the least accusatory way I could.

Andropoulos, the better actor of the two, looked at Streiker with wide eyes

"No. I . . . we . . . didn't, Captain Wright. What's wrong with them?"

"They are all rotten right through. They won't hold a cupful of water. Did you know, Captain Streiker?"

Streiker averted his eyes. "Well . . . I did look at them, but . . . er . . . I didn't think they were all that bad."

My job was to pass judgment on the ship, not on the captain or the owner's rep. "Okay, gentlemen," I said decisively, "rather than continue my survey and run up unnecessary expenses, I can tell you now that in her present condition, I will not recommend that this vessel be placed in line for entry into the U.K Club; she is unseaworthy."

"But, Captain, we do not intend to use those ballast tanks . . .so-o-o?"

He knew about the tanks, I surmised. Greasy bastard. I wonder what he'll try next.

"My decision has been made, Mr. Andropoulos. You are not sailing in this ship, correct?" Without waiting for an answer, I asked the captain. "Captain Streiker, I presume you too knew about the ballast tanks. Would you have proceeded to sea with the ship in this condition?"

Poor Streiker! He had to get off this ride somewhere.

Streiker got up from the table and looked across at the owner's representative. "I knew you'd never get away with it." Turning to me he said, "Of course not. I'm only here to make the number up. I'm going back to Germany tomorrow." He left the saloon and went into his room.

An embarrassing silence followed, felt more especially by me on behalf of Captain Streiker. I had sat down and continued to scribble a few salient notes in my notebook.

Mr. Andropoulos cleared his throat. "Captain Wright, I'm sure you know what kind of a position this puts me in?" I went on writing in my book. "Look, perhaps we could come to some kind of arrangement. I really don't want to offend you, sir, but I have certain . . .er . . . arrangements I can make without raising any eyebrows." I was looking at him now. "For instance I could offer you – and your wife – a ten day cruise to the Caribbean on our cruise ship and $2000 to spend."

The look on his face told me that he wished he had not made the offer – he already knew the answer. He didn't mention the bribe again but saw me quietly off the ship. He thanked me for attending, and then hardly daring to broach the subject again, he said, almost under his breath, "You won't mention my proposition in your report?"

"I'm only interested in the ship, Mr. Andropoulos. When those shell plates have been refitted to Lloyds Surveyor's satisfaction, there is a possibility that your ship could complete a transpacific voyage just as she is, without further incident, but there is always the chance that something would happen and she wouldn't make it. I will not take chances on ships and men. Sorry, Mr. Andropoulos." I didn't really feel sorry for him. I could almost hear his owners telling him not to fail them, because they had some hot deal made in Korea or Hong Kong to sell her along with the 22,000 tons of scrap steel she had laden on board in San Francisco. *Use every means at your disposal to get the surveyor to go along with you.*

*

Several months later I happened to be in San Francisco and bumped into one of the Admiralty Lawyers who represented the Club who had asked me to survey Gryphen.

"Hi Peter. How are you?" Charlie Ross slapped me on the back just as I sat down to lunch on the Wharf. "Do you remember Gryphen – down in Ensenada?"

"All too well," I replied with a hint of wariness.

"Well, without going into all the gory details, how did you find her?" I gave him a five minute extract of my report to the Club recommending that in her present condition, I would not endorse her on account of her lack of seaworthiness.

Charlie sat for a minute or two frowning into his soup. "Funny" he significantly muttered. "Our surveyor gave Gryphen a clean bill of health. I believe she took a full load of scrap to – somewhere in the far east."

I was surprised, but not scandalously so. such scams are probably commonplace. "I'm damned glad nothing happened," I said before leaving Charlie, "that would have placed me in the position of being a whistle-blower."

*

# The Recalcitrant Cleric

*The Priest and his Small Wooden Box*

Perhaps one of the most adventurous assignments I have ever been given was during the early autumn of 1989. At that time I was a Marine Investigator living in Long Beach, California. One afternoon, Canadian interests called me from Vancouver, B.C., and asked if I would be willing to travel to Lake Athabasca, in Saskatchewan, the following day to investigate the nature, cause and extent of loss of a number of steel barges loaded with household and grocery goods under tow, that had been cut loose during a storm and run ashore on one, or several, of the numerous small islands that lie mid-lake toward the eastern end of Lake Athabasca.

Without much hesitation I agreed to travel up the following day without stipulations: I trusted the Canadian lawyers. Instructions were simple: proceed to Vancouver, B.C., thence to Fort McMurray, Alberta (at the western end of the Lake) contact Paul's Float Plane Company and fly to the site of the wreck.

The flight from Los Angeles to Vancouver was relatively normal: by today's standards it was luxuriously flawless. Fort McMurray, however, was not the most frequently visited city in Western Canada. Many people had never heard of the place, for it boasted nothing but the largest trout in the world and the equipment with which to catch it.

I arrived late in the afternoon, found a hotel and called Paul's Float Plane Company. I had been warned by Vancouver agents that Mr. Paul was French Canadian and for some reason didn't like the English.

"Heh."

"Is that Mr. Paul?"

"Who wants to know?"

*Good God!* I thought, *A French Canadian standoff.* "This is Peter Wright, the surveyor . . . ."

"I know. I know," he interrupted, "I don't fly any more tonight."

"No, I understand that, Mr. Paul. What time shall I see you tomorrow?"

After a short pause, during which I could him muttering something to someone, "After mass, about ten o'clock." He hung up abruptly.

I spent about two hours that evening gazing in wonderment at an early display of Aurora Borealis. The temperature dropped to near freezing that night, a significant atmospheric modification from the day's high of seventy Fahrenheit.

Sunday dawned bright and clear. I hoped that Mr. Paul's visit to pay his respects to his maker had improved his mood, and with the forthcoming long flight an hour away, had changed his impression of the English – particularly *this* Englishman.

Mr. Paul, like every good mechanic, was standing on the float checking gauges and valves when I said, "Bon Jour, Monsieur Paul." Apparently he didn't hear me. "Good morning Mr. Paul." I repeated. He did hear me, for he stopped doing what he was doing for a moment, and half turned.

*Must have missed going to communion*, I thought. "Looks like a nice day for a flight over the lake, eh?" I ventured.

This time he looked directly at me and pointed to the cabin door of the HUSKIE III float plane which lay open, but didn't say a word. Obediently I threw my flight bag behind the passenger seat and climbed in after it. Reassured by the neatness of the cockpit and the general cleanliness, I hoped that if our friendship didn't exactly blossom, that we could engage in some kind of conversation.

Unlike a wheeled aircraft on a runway where the brakes are left on until sufficient thrust has built up, seaplanes start to move as soon as the propeller turns. It appears, therefore, that the plane travels many miles before the pilot pulls the stick back and the floats leave the surface. During the protracted takeoff I thought it better not to try and engage the pilot in any form of conversation. We headed east, with the sun halfway to its zenith. Below lay Lake Athabasca like a shimmering sea of quicksilver under a cloudless sky. The south shore, clearly defined by a sandy beach that stretched as far as the eye could see, looked a lot like the Northwest Territories; vast stretches of scrubland interspersed with numerous lakes which reflected the sun's rays and brilliantly lit up the inside of the cockpit.

"What's our ETA?" I enquired in a voice loud enough to be audible over the roar of the engines. I then noted he was wearing a set of earphones and decided not to embarrass myself further by trying to make conversation.

I rummaged through my work attaché case and pulled out all the documents I had on the casualty. There was precious little. The storm had erupted during the night of last Friday about ninety miles west of Fond du Lac. The only map I had was a fisherman's guide to the Best Trout fishing in the World. The scale was accurate enough for me to get a reasonable geographical fix on where the stranded barges might be. They appeared to be among several islands fairly close inshore where the north shore dipped toward the Fond du Lac narrows, about twenty miles south by east of Uranium City.

My eye suddenly caught a glimpse of something out on the lake – to my left – just emerging from the bright patch of sunlight. It was a motor tugboat heading for the north shore. The north shore was barely visible, but I could see well enough that there were several inlets with some kind of waterfront structures. I wondered if this was the tug in question – *Le Bijou* – the one which abandoned the barges. In an hours time I would know.

Close to lunch time, my gracious pilot removed a huge ham and egg sandwich from a plastic bag, and proceeded to munch. Thoroughly disenchanted with his behavior, I muttered fuck him under my breath and consoled myself that the flight must very soon be over.

A change in the tone of the engine told me we were descending. Right ahead I picked out the outlines of several small islets, each about half a mile in diameter. Sure enough, the one with about six barges lying at an angle on what appeared to be stony beach must be it.

At about 200 feet altitude I nudged the pilot and asked him to circle the island so that I could see the general outlay and take some pictures. Without hesitation he leveled out and went around twice, then swooped low over the southern tip of the islet, turned north and landed perfectly on the east side of what turned out to be Eagle Island. It was one o'clock in the afternoon. The weather was calm and the lake like a mirror. Someone had put together a makeshift floating dock with some steel barrels and 2 inch x 10 inch planking, but I didn't see any workmen, neither could I see any debris from the barges for that seemed to be on the other side of the island, a couple of hundred feet over a slight rise.

Focusing on what my next course of action would be, I lowered myself gingerly onto the jury dock, pulled duffle bag and attaché case down and started over the dune to look for the rest of the salvage crew. The first spectacle that I beheld was thirty or forty noisy ravens raucously screeching, attacking some cartons of foodstuff – and each other, and millions of blackflies which swarmed away from the food toward me – apparently the only human being. At that moment the roar of the Huskie's twelve cylinder engines brought me to the terrifying realization that my stalwart friend, Mr. Paul, was deserting me. I knew he had planned this move. I doubt very much if he saw me shaking my fist in rage at him, he was already a mile down-lake. *God damned son-of-a-bitch . . . . . .!* I had to admit that I had been in tricky situations before in many countries, but I had never been in one like this.

I am a great believer in the twelve steps of any personal recovery program, so beginning with "I am powerless over . . . " I pretended that being on this island by myself in the middle of a lake in a foreign country was just where I was supposed to be.

I had brought my binoculars and was able to ascertain that there was no visible wreckage or flotsam on any of the other two islands. Back at the western beach, where most of the flotsam lay strewn along five hundred feet of sandy shingle, the ravens were having a high old time. Cartons of corn flakes, bags of rice and a hundred other packages of food stuffs, including plastic tubs of margarine and butter, were being plundered by seemingly ravenous, winged maniacs. I had to sit down and watch the antics of some of these birds. In their frenzy to get at the contents of the tubs of margarine, a few of the ravens had driven their beaks right through the tightly fitting plastic lid, which in turn had firmly affixed itself to their bulbous walnut-shaped beaks thereby rendering these fiercely carnivorous birds into comical, waddling avian clowns.

I took a quick look at the rest of the wreckage and discovered that there were, in fact, six barges; two made fast to each other in tandem and two more single barges farther on down the beach. Each barge contained two piggyback, forty-foot rail containers, two of which had collapsed allowing their contents to spill, some on the barge, the rest into the lake. The remaining containers were damaged but intact. At least three of the barges were resting on the bottom and had probably bilged, for the surrounding water for hundreds of yards was oil slicked. It smelled and looked like household furnace oil.

There was a great deal of work to be done, but that could start tomorrow when, I sincerely hoped, a salvage crew would join me. *Sufficient unto the day is the evil thereof,* I reminded myself. *Where would I sleep? Damn that bloody Frenchman. If this wasn't the French Canadian's ultimate revenge!* I knew it would be cold, so if I could find a place off the ground I'd be happier. After scrounging through the part contents of one of the collapsed containers I found a roll of plastic and a couple of furniture remover's blankets. I made a hammock out of ten or so sheets of the plastic and suspended it a couple of feet above the ground between four trees and prepared myself for an uneventful night.

No cloud cover allowed free radiation and I guessed that it went down to 10 or 15 Fahrenheit. The blankets kept me warm but the noise of the stranded barges grinding on the rocks I found discomfiting.

With a great roar of high powered engines, the salvage crew arrived by boat at six o'clock the following morning and tied up at the makeshift dock where I had been stranded. Six Indian workers and six technicians, including a young marine engineer representing the London Salvage Association, and five skilled riggers: a good team. I was surprised not to see a surveyor representing the tow company's interests. I found out later that the head rigger filled in for that job – he asked if he could copy my notes!

In the manner of Stanley and Livingstone, Red, the head rigger, greeted me on his arrival, "Captain Wright, I presume," in a broad Saskatchewan brogue. "Did that goddam Frenchman leave you here without warning? He hasn't done that since the last Englishman he ferried." He laughed. "We are not Catholic, but we don't work on Sunday either. Where would you like to start?"

"We need a couple of mobile cranes, ten ton limit will do, and a couple of D.9 tractors. I suggest we transfer as much salvageable cargo onto barges, take it to Uranium City, transload it into containers and deliver it to Fond du Lac.

Red said, "All on the way; ought to be here tomorrow. How long to you reckon?"

How would I know? I thought for a minute: "Couple of weeks," I said. Red turned on his heel and within five minute he had his men collecting sound, if not too badly waterlogged or physically damaged goods and stacking them at a selected spot on the beach

My job was simply to evaluate the loss, and to determine the cause and the nature of the loss. The testimony of the tugboat skipper would have been implicit had he agreed to talk to me and allowed me to read his deck and engine log books. Before he left, however, he had spoken to Red and given him a rough outline of what had happened during the storm, and original manifests of all the cargo laden on board the barges at Fort McMurray.

Captain Raoul Matthieu of *Bijou,* reported that the barometer had started to fall before he left Fort McMurray, but that he had no idea of the intensity of the approaching low. Atmospheric pressure then rapidly dropped and before he knew it he had a force 8 wind blowing from the southeast. He shortened the tow and proceeded at a moderate speed. One of the bridles on the lead barge parted and the barge started to slew and yaw putting a tremendous strain on the other bridle. For fear of losing the entire tow, and possibly his tugboat, he maneuvered around the western end of Eagle Island and slipped the entire tow. Fortunately he was close enough to the island that the lead barge ran ashore, anchoring itself, causing the remaining barges to follow suit. The only question unanswered was, what was that tug's horsepower? But I could get that from Lloyd's.

Among the cargo being transferred, were twelve snowmobiles, all of which had sustained physical damage or minor scratches, twelve glass-fronted refrigerated display cabinets, all damaged, and twelve four-wheeled ATV's, some slightly damaged. There were also a couple of large crates of household goods, furniture: chests of drawers, boxes of books and so on. They would all bear further scrutiny and some repair after delivery to the owners.

I was busy writing up some notes when one of the riggers came over and suggested that I'd better go and take a look at something. The "something" was a steel banded wooden chest containing some bottles, magnetic tapes, sacred literature and rosary beads, all addressed to Père

Francois LeClerc, Léglise Sacré Coer, Fond du Lac, Saskatchewan, Canada. Water had entered the box. Everything was wet.

I searched the manifest and found Father LeClerc. In addition to a snowmobile and an ATV, assuredly for delivering the Last Sacraments to some peasant living in an outlying farm in midwinter, there was:

> One (1) wooden box of stout construction, said to contain
> Two (2) -1 litre bottles of Italian wine,
> Six (6) pairs of rosary beads of glass and metal chain construction
> Two (2) missals printed in Latin and French
> Two (2) magnetic tapes (Sony) of sixty minuest, marked "The Pope."

I suspected that all of these items held some personal significance to Father LeClerc. I therefore closed the box and sealed it with one of my own seals, and set it aside for further investigation.

Meanwhile the salvage work went on, both the riggers and Indian laborers performing amazing feats of ingenuity, bearing in mind the difficult geographical conditions under which they were obliged to work. All the barges were emptied and the contents placed on a sound barge from Uranium City and taken there for transportation to Fond du Lac.

Toward the end of my investigation, I spent an entire day in that now ghostlike place. Once a thriving city of several thousand Cree Indians, most of whom worked in the uranium mine and others in the laboratory where the uranium was isolated from its other component chemicals, both the town and the mine shut down when the discovery of a richer field was made on the other side of the lake, about one hundred miles to the south. Within a few months every house became vacant, not a car could be seen on the wide, fir-lined, unpaved street, and every window was boarded up. All that remained was a hamburger café where they barbequed moose and elk hamburgers, and a small, fully staffed hospital; I am not sure if the two establishments were gastronomically connected, although I have to admit that I've never tasted better meat. It was in one of these vacated houses that we, the salvage crew and I, spent our nights. The days had become overcast, producing a few snow flurries, and the nights were cold! The hospital very kindly loaned us a few blankets; we may otherwise never have completed the salvage operation.

It was in my "office" in Uranium City that I met Father LeClerc. He had traveled from Fond du Lac unannounced, to claim his belongings. Except for the black buttoned-up robe, through the throat of which peeped a starched *dog-collar,* he may well have stepped right out of the pages of one of Agatha Christie's novels – the image of Hercule Poirot, the fussy little Belgian detective, with round, gold-rimmed glasses, his head adorned with a black, soup-plate shaped hat.

He introduced himself and pumped my hand with an excess of self-consciousness. "Captain Wright, I 'ave bin looking for you all morning, to Fort.MacMurray, to the . . .the . . .island, an' 'ere you are! So what 'as happened to my . . .'ow you say . . . ATV, an' my box from La Pape, ze Pope? Zere was . . .*un orage* . .a storm, *non?*"

I interrupted what I guessed would have been a long harangue about his recent maritime loss, by holding up both my hands in supplication. "Sorry, Father. Let me explain what happened, and where you and I stand. Where I stand with the insurance company, and where you stand with the insurance company. Understand?"

Relieved not to have to go on grabbing at his broken English and trying to translate it into English I would understand, he nodded.

"There was a storm on Lake Athabasca last Friday a week ago." I pointed my index finger toward heaven. The priest smiled thinly.

"In order to save the crew of his tugboat from being dragged ashore and possibly being drowned, the captain let the tow go." LeClerk held up a finger.

"Yes, Father?"

"Isn't it ze captain's job to save the cargo?"

"Not at the expense of human life," I said, and watched his expression. He nodded his head reluctantly and looked at the floor but remained silent."

"It so happens that your ATV and your snowmobile are here, ashore, waiting to be shipped to your home. I have already examined them. There are several scratches and dents to the fenders and exterior protective plastic, all of which are listed in my report, and which you may now examine. They both got wet but were not immersed. I have been able to fire them both up. Okay?"

"Do I get new ones?" He asked hopefully.

"Based on my report, and the photographs that will accompany it, you will get an allowance for replacing decals and paint work, possibly a new fender on the ATV. But so far as I could see neither has been damaged sufficiently to warrant a unit replacement. Do you understand all I've said?"

Once again he nodded his head. Still looking at the photographs I had given him, he held one up showing a dent in the front fender of the Honda ATV. "'Ow about zees one?" he asked. I shook my head without making eye contact. I was not going to get into a shouting match about a $25 dent.

We sat in silence for a minute; he, no doubt, wondering how God could have allowed this to happen; me, trying not to feel like God.

"Zere was also a box from ze Vatican; a personal gift to me from ze Pope. Is zat also damaged?"

I should have thought that the box would have been first on his list. A worldly priest?

"I have that right here," I said, and went over to the corner, picked the box up and placed it on the table. "Please open it up,Father, and tell me if there anything missing."

Father LeClerc, who had now removed his clerical hat, reached over and cut the seal with my knife, and gingerly opened the box as though it might now contain something fiendish.

"Oh – oh – oh!" He ejected in disappointment. "Zey are all wet." He picked up a missal and delicately tried to open the pages. "Zeez are irreplaceable." He continued to remove the contents. The magnetic tapes expelled a drop or two of water. The labels on the bottles of wine were legible, but only just. The rosary beads seemed to be sound.

"Alors, Captain Wright. 'ow do you place a value on zese items, *hein?* Zose tapes are recordings of some conversations I 'ad with ze Pope. Ze wine is especially pressed for ze Pope. It takes two years to settle. Both my breviaries (missals) were signed by ze Pope."

I knew it was coming. How does one place a dollar value on items of sentimental value? I was not very good in this sort of situation. I tended to dredge up guilt and lose my train of thought. Except for my refusal to become a priest during my school days, I had only a blurred idea of why I was attacked by this pervasive emotion when someone was pleading or arguing a point upon which I agreed with the pleader.

"Father LeClerc," I said in my most conciliatory manner, "I deal with three dimensional objects, including people, during my investigations. Attaching an emotion to an object gives it another dimension – a fourth dimension, for which, so far as I am concerned, there is no monetary value."

He looked quizzically at me, apparently not understanding my English. "Look," I said. "Your breviaries for instance . . ." I stopped myself from using the metaphor I had in mind. "Excuse me, Father. Let me try again. A photograph of . . .say, your mother." The priest turned and looked sharply at me. "That picture, but for the actual cost of printing and the cost of the paper, has no value to me at all – not the slightest, but for you it may have enormous sentimental value, but it still has no monetary value." I looked for a spark of acquiescence, a glimmer from those wary eyes. All I saw was a flash of anger. I wondered if I had put my foot in it again. Seems I had.

"My mother?" He exclaimed in some alarm. "Why are you talking about my mother? What has she to do with my breviaries and my wine?"

I held up both hands in surrender. "Just a minute, Father, I was using your mother's picture metaphorically: I was merely trying to demonstrate the difference between actual value and sentimental value."

While I was speaking, the Reverend was placing items that had been removed from the back, back where they came from. I was feeling rather uncomfortable because all I had accomplished was to make the consignee mad, instead of comforted that his loss was being taken care of. I didn't make the bloody rules, I thought. Perhaps I could do some damage control.

"Father LeClerc," I said touching him on the arm, trying an old therapist trick. "I can suggest an offer that might be satisfactory to both you and the insurance company."

He paused and glanced suspiciously at me. "*Alors,* 'ow much?"

I did some quick thinking. "Even though the wine has not been contaminated, except by having been shaken during the passage," I said, " I'll admit that it has become less attractive because the labels are smudged, therefore I'll suggest that the underwriters allow you a couple of bottles of the wine of your choice, say $60.00 each." I watched for his immediate reaction; there was none. "The breviaries are ruined, that I know, but there are people who do that kind of work – dry out books that have been saturated." I started to tell him about an air shipment of valuable architectural sketches for the Getty Museum in Los Angeles that had sat out in a heavy shower at Heathrow, but decided not to bother. The priest was no longer in any mood to listen to fancy tales of recovery.

By now he had replaced all the articles in the box and was closing it. I felt the futility of trying to convince this cleric that life can be unwittingly cruel, and that the cold comfort of a sympathetic adjuster's recognition of the complexities of the problem, is better than no comfort at all. "I'm sorry, Father, that you have sustained a loss that cannot be repaired in full. I shall point out the magnitude of your loss in my report. I hope you have a favorable response." We shook hands, and he was gone.

There was much to be done on Eagle Island. The heating oil was eventually pumped into another barge and taken on to Fond du Lac. On the tenth day the barges were empty. Lying like beached whales on the shingle shore, we faced the daunting problem of getting them back to Fort MacMurray. By hitching a 3" steel hawser onto each barge in turn, the D.9 was able to drag four of them five or six feet farther up the steep beach. Our assumption, was that the bottom damage to each barge, if any, would be confined to the lee side. However a subsequent thorough examination of the bottom plates revealed that two barges had sustained repairable indentations and holes. After welding the holes closed, the barges were pushed back into the lake, all air vents and tank sounding pipes were sealed closed and one and a half pounds of air was introduced through an air pipe by means of a compressor..

The last barge, too far offshore to examine, seemed to be floating. A tug from Fort MacMurray arrived on the eleventh day and took them in tow.

We all gave a mighty cheer as the tug got under way and the barges, in tight formation, began to move off to the west. Our self congratulations were somewhat dashed five minutes later. The last barge appeared to have been fast to the bottom. As the towline took the weight, it jerked into motion as it was released from what we presumed was a rock – a big rock – a big hole. The tugboat skipper saw it coming and dispatched a man to let the barge go. It sank thirty yards offshore. We marked it with two orange buoys.

I thanked the salvage crew for their diligent efforts, and especially the young Newcastle engineer who had solved the true salvage dilemma by refloating the barges. The beach, upon which most of the flotsam had landed, now looked fairly pristine. The ravens had gone, no doubt wondering where those strange "beak traps" had come from, and what sort of message they brought!

I spent my last night in Saskatchewan in the same room in which I had had my discussion with Father Le Clerc. Wondering how this naïve cleric would fare wallowing about in an ocean of Admiralty Law, I didn't sleep very well.

A very different Paul, my pilot, greeted me at the Uranium City landing stage at eight o'clock the next morning. He even said, "Good Morning."

As soon as we took off, he offered me coffee from his thermos. I accepted gratefully, for it was now bitterly cold, and with some surprise. Wonder what he wants?

"Everything back there okay," he asked. I thought it an unusual question.

"In what way?"

"I mean, how much cargo was lost?"

I wasn't about to tell him that. "Oh," I casually said, a fair amount of groceries were abandoned, but all-in-all the loss was reasonably small considering the circumstances."

"What about Father Francis' belongings?"

It took me a minute to realize who he was talking about. "Father LeClerc?"

"Yes, he's my brother you know." No, I didn't know, and that bit of information put me on my guard. "I see," I said, "Well, he lost some souvenirs the Pope had blessed. Very sad really, because they are irreplaceable, especially the conversations on tape. But even so, if they are dried in diatomaceous earth, they may not be a total loss."

We sat in silence for a short while, each of us thinking about Fr. LeClerc's loss, he offensively, me defensively.

"D'you think a lawyer would be a good idea?" Paul tentatively asked.

I didn't want to answer him. Lawyers are not honest enough when it comes to a question of actual values. "Whatever the good Father wants to do is okay with me," I said.

A week later I had a call from my principal in Vancouver.

"We have almost got an international crisis on our hands. Did you ever say that the items blessed by the Pope and donated to that Cleric were *valueless?*" I had an idea that this would come back to haunt me. There must be a lawyer involved.

"Well . . .yes, I did, but only out of context." I explained how I demonstrated the difference between monetary value and sentimental value.

"Okay, Peter, you know what happens to a simple case when lawyers intervene. We may need you up here for a deposition, but let us not look on the dismal side." I thanked him for the assignment and promised him a full report by the week's end.

At the end of my report I remembered to insert a little wisdom from Saint Luke:

*Woe unto you, Lawyers! For ye have taken away the Key of knowledge.*

# Nigel Trask

## *I meet an unbelieving, changeless Englishman*

When I was a small boy growing up in a narrow-minded Irish Catholic family, I was told that profanity of any kind was a precursor to the road to hell, and atheistical, or any word or phrase which indicated a disbelief in God was considered profane. In secret talks with my mother, she explained that atheists were ambassadors of the Devil, evil mongers. Later on, when I was a prospective priest at a Catholic boarding school, I learned that there was no such thing as an atheist - that it was a contradiction in terms. My spiritual advisor at the time often told the story of a German atheist he knew in Cologne who became the butt of the local kids' pranks. One night they climbed on his roof and lowered a fiendish effigy, attached to which were tin cans, down his chimney. He is reported to have almost jumped out of his skin, yelling, "*Oh my God, it's the Devil.*" I thought the incident funny but certainly not conclusive proof that there was no such thing as an atheist.

During the next phase of my life, the one spent at sea and around ships, the subject of atheism seldom, if ever, entered into any of my conversations. Before proceeding further with my tale, however, I will mention what I consider to be an important factor when talking about atheism. I knew many sailors, quite a few soldiers and airmen during the war, who never once expressed their disbelief in some form of deity. My own conclusion to that anomaly, if you wish to categorize it as such, is that sailors, soldiers and airmen are constantly in harm's way and must therefore believe in *something spiritual – a God of his or her understanding.*

During my recovery from alcoholism, God was a constant source of inspiration. I prayed that he would continue to support my tenuous recovery from that awful disease, and I took for granted, without any consideration of the philosophical approach to my entreaties, that since I continued to stay sober, that He was my ally. It was at this stage of my spiritual growth that I met Nigel, a resident of the far northern California town where I would eventually go to retire.

Before I met Nigel, however, I met Marietta, his wife, behind the jewelry counter of a department store. I was thinking about buying a set of earrings for my wife.

"You're English, aren't you?" Dressed in a black suit, white *petit-point* satin blouse buttoned at the neck, black stockings and patent high heeled shoes, she immediately became the focus of my attention. I looked up from the display case to get a better glimpse. From a narrow face, two knowing eyes looked into mine. Accentuating her pallor, a pair of provocative bright red lips twitched slightly. While I mentally undressed her in an attempt to determine the shape of the bosom that swelled beneath the jacket, and the curve of hip and bottom, equally teasing, she busied herself getting the earrings which were becoming less and less important to me.

"Er . . . yes I am," I said, experiencing the bitter/sweetness and drenching reality of sobriety.

"My husband Nigel is also English. Would you like to meet him?"

Unwilling to allow the latest object of my fantasy sail away like a ship in the night, I said I would, and gave her my card. I left the counter and turned to take another look at this woman who had captivated my imagination. Those eyes had passed a message to me – an appeal.

The following morning, Nigel telephoned me, and we made arrangements to meet for coffee – at MacDonald's of all places. "Why there," I'd asked him. "Because it's cheaper," he said:.There is nothing worse than a cheap Englishman.

*

I found Nigel behind the *Wall Street Journal.* Apart from the incongruity of his reading material and the stark vulgarity of the establishment, I was able to pick him out instantly – blue blazer with brass buttons, gray flannel pants, and an ascot just visible behind a plain white shirt.

"Peter, nice to see you." He proffered a thin, cold hand. There was no life in his grip. An ill-fitting gray toupee crowned an intelligent, pallid face from which an aquiline nose protruded. His left eye was missing and had been replaced by an unfocussed, disturbingly off-center glass replica. He didn't attempt to get up. Instinctively I knew the man was ill, and from the expression in his right eye, angry and defiant.

We did the fellow-expatriates thing and asked each other about our origins. I gave him a brief outline of my life leaving out some of the juicier bits. When I told him I was born in Liverpool, he uttered a noise which sounded like "ugh." I knew then that he and I would never to get along.

Nigel's life, rather duller than mine I thought, started in Calcutta, India, in 1935. The only son of British colonial parents, the father in His Majesty's Service, he grew up in care of an *amah* until he was ten years of age. After that the Jesuits at nearby Bhātpara College continued his education with the hope of preparing him for whatever vicissitudes life might offer. At the age of eighteen, thoroughly fed up with what was left of British India, Nigel joined the army in 1954 simply to get a free passage back to the United Kingdom.

He briefly mentioned an earlier marriage and some children, but moved on quickly, just as I in the same manner, did not dwell on my three failed partnerships. It saved us both from making up excuses and generally lying. Nonetheless, from the few details he afforded me, I gathered that his prior family life had been fierce. Although he did not tell me the exact cause of the loss of his left eye, I suspected that it may have been incidental to a passionate marital altercation.

His voice was distinctly Oxford, acerbic and supercilious. Our commonalities included sharing the same dual nationality, British/ American, speaking the language with the same accent, and having attended Catholic colleges. Our personal differences were more subtle: I had mellowed - he had not; I was a lapsed Catholic, and he, I would find out later, was an atheist.

When it came time to leave, he struggled to his feet with the aid of a silver-topped cane and handed me his business card. "Call me," he said, and climbed into an ancient, but immaculate, Volvo. The abruptness of his departure left me wondering if I had in some way offended him, but I concluded that it was part of his natural rudeness. The plain white business card contained two pieces of information, his name and his profession – *Hypothecator*. After consulting a dictionary, I learned that he was *a person who pledges property or goods as security for a debt without surrendering ownership*. I am still not sure precisely what he did for a living, but I suspect that he was a real estate agent. We met several times for coffee after that, but never again at McDonald's.

I learned that his wife, Marietta, had suffered a terrible tragedy twenty or so years ago, from which she never fully recovered. She, her previous husband and their two sons, had fallen under the spell of charismatic Jim Jones, and had gone with him and nine-hundred other followers to Guyana. After listening for several months to the doctrine of The Temple of God, Marietta became suspicious of Jones' true motives. Unsuccessful in her attempts to persuade her husband and the boys to leave with her, she escaped on one of the last planes to leave before Jim Jones induced nine hundred of his disciples to drink cyanide-laced Kool-Aid. She learned of the death of her family after returning to California. I wondered if she had ever sought counsel, or whether she still carried that burden around with her. Perhaps I'd seen it in her eyes.

Nigel and I mainly discussed typical English ex-patriates stuff: the government under Margaret Thatcher; the cruelty of the English Public School system, and the distressing absence of "Bangers & Mash" from the menus of our former colony. One morning he broached the subject of religion.

"How much of that religious crap they pummel into you at that fancy Dominican school did you take away to sea with you, and how much do you still believe?" I wondered at the ferocity of his verbal attack." Do you still believe that there is a God in Heaven, the same one who is supposed to have made you?"

The derision in his voice became less irritating as I remembered my own faltering faith during some of the dark episodes in my life, the times I had called for help and He had done nothing about it. Religion was not a subject I relished because at that time I harbored heretical thoughts about God. I was happy being who I was without trying to explain things to others.

"Damn it all Nigel, you know as well as I do there is no such thing as an atheist. If you spent seven years at a Jesuit college, you can't possibly be a non-believer. Atheism is a fad – a way of shirking responsibility." Once again my mind shifted to the seedy days of my own escapades and the way I had manipulated my religious beliefs to suit myself. *Hypocritical bastard!* I knew that Nigel held the trump card in this Godly game of words --senseless deaths, famine, disease, all of which, he would advocate, should have been prevented by God. All I had in my hand was a fraction of faith, a lot of fear, and my mother's voice in my young ear, "Don't forget to go to mass when you're in them foreign parts."

"Come down to our meeting next Sunday afternoon," Nigel suggested, "you may be surprised how we face life without a god."

As I made my way down to the Atheist Assembly Hall situated below a tall railroad trestle, echoes of strident Catholic fulminations came to mind: *thou shalt not . . . walk by a Protestant church . . . enter into any dealings with other religions . . . ever take the name of the lord thy God in vain.* I was inviting hell fire and brimstone just thinking about atheism.

In a small corrugated iron shed, thirty-seven people had already assembled when Nigel and I arrived. The smell of cigarette smoke and stale coffee reminded me of those small rooms where I attended meetings of Alcoholics Anonymous, and where members of that fellowship focused on hopes for the future through a Higher Power. The atmosphere in this building which lay one hundred and fifty feet below the Southern Pacific railroad trestle, brought to mind images of Trotsky and Lenin plotting the Russian revolution.

They knew Nigel, but were suspicious of me. I viewed the assembly through a depressing, yellow/green aura. I felt no joy here. There seemed to be no structure to the meeting. The subject under discussion was the Bible, and the object, so far as I could tell, was to ridicule its contents. Everybody was talking; nobody was listening. After thirty minutes I couldn't take it any longer, and told Nigel I was leaving. We spoke no more about the people who had found a way to live without God.

"Either you believe, or you don't, Nigel. It's as simple as that. I prefer to acknowledge the presence of a power greater than myself who had something to do with our creation, than to support the idea that we arrived here from the primordial ooze by accident."

"But you have absolutely no evidence to the contrary except the ramblings of a few dotty old men who fantasized their dreams in the Bible." Nigel paused for minute. "Peter, have you ever experienced God's work during your life?" I knew that I had, but I had no desire to try to explain. I was alive and well, and I knew that I should be dead

I spent many evenings in the company of Nigel and Marietta. We talked of India, Pakistan, of Oxford and – cricket. Marietta seldom contributed to the conversation, but sat apart, crocheting. I imagined she had little to say about God. The loss of her husband and two sons was probably a sacrifice she would never come to terms with. She seldom looked at Nigel, and on the few occasions she glanced in his direction, I sensed nothing but icy hatred. I felt a pang of compassion for both of them; I had been there before.

On the last afternoon that we would ever simply have tea together, Nigel arrived home a little later than originally promised. His usual entrance, often theatrical, quoting a line or two from Shakespeare, was wordless today. He stood by the front window for a moment silhouetted against the yellowing light of a stormy March evening. I noticed that he seemed to be more stooped than the last time I had seen him.

"Bad day Nigel?" I said, to break the silence, and cursed myself immediately for not being more observant – less flippant.

"That bloody Indian doctor tells me I have about three weeks to live." I knew that he was ill, but this unexpected announcement floored me. I looked at Marietta and saw her features harden, but I also saw her eyes glisten. I don't think she was crying.

I said, "What the hell are you talking about?" He glanced briefly at me then made eye contact with his wife.

"You didn't tell him, did you?" It was almost an accusation. Without taking her eyes off him, Marietta slowly shook her head. Eyebrows raised, mouth slightly open, her face was the picture of concerned innocence. I think she had just seen the dawn of a new life. Caught up in this climactic moment in the lives of these two people, I sensed clearly the fear, hatred and distrust that had developed between them over the past twenty years, distilled into a drop of true understanding

- he was dying, and glad of it, and she was elated, for she would soon be free.

Nigel broke a breathless silence. "I've had colon cancer for eighteen months. Every so often the doctors try out a new form of chemo on me. This afternoon I refused to be their guinea pig any longer. I told them they could shove their drugs up their respective arses." He smiled thinly and removed his pathetic toupee. Making a point of avoiding any form of contact with Marietta, he took my arm and steered me toward the fire blazing in the hearth. "Do you know, Peter, I haven't felt this good in years." He turned around to warm his bottom against the fire. "Now I'm going to find out what those chaps on death row down at San Quentin feel like."

Marietta called me that evening. "As one of my dearest friends, and one of the few men I can trust, would you devote some time to Nigel whenever you can? It's a tough thing to ask, but I know you understand." How could I refuse?

The following day Nigel apologized for what he described as *an unhappy domestic interlude.* "Marietta tells me that you are going to come over every day until . . . I cross the Styx." I heard him chuckle. "Jolly nice of you, old boy."

I was surprised to see Nigel weaken so fast. Although never hale and hearty, the deterioration in his physical condition was measurable daily. I wondered how long his brain would function.

While he was still lucid, Nigel told me of a life of acute unhappiness. Unloved, seemingly unwanted, he held onto his natural moral fibre, but he didn't call it faith. In their belief that God could and would solve all man's problems, the Jesuits had failed to build Nigel's self worth. It was the unadulterated, unrelieved internal chaos in Nigel's life that caused him to push God out of his belief system. I fully understood. I led the life of an incorrigible drunk for twenty years and knew the sounds, the taste and smell of despair.

What I noticed emerging from his stories was a plaintive cry for help. He always asked me for my opinion.

Late one afternoon after I had propped Nigel up so that he could watch M*A*S*H, a show that seemed to bring him alive, as I turned to leave I heard him call my name.

In a voice barely audible he said. "Peter, I've been thinking about your God." He stared piercingly at me with his good eye; the socket of his left eye was now covered with a black patch. "Tell me again what you think."

I think he was pleading, trying in his own way to *even the playing field* just in case there really was a God waiting for him on the other side. What do you say to a dying man? If he is in pain, you give him drugs, but what if he's afraid of the unknown? You have to tell him something to allay his fears. You try to ease him through the final moments of his life until he no longer cares. I cast my mind back to the occasions when I nearly lost my life. During each incident, my only thought was wishing not to die like my father with lungs filled with sea water. God did not enter my mind. Years later, squatting under a freeway in San Francisco with the city's forgotten homeless, I had had to make a choice – walk out into the traffic or live. People told me that I had chosen God - I believed them. Nigel should have been talking with a man of God, not a formerly drunken old sailor.

"I happen to think there is a God, Nigel," I said, trying hard to remember what St. Thomas Aquinas had to say about the existence of God. Then it occurred to me that plain logic might calm his quivering nerves. "You remember that meeting under the railway trestle, you know – those weird people who didn't believe in God; there were thirty-seven of them, remember? Well, there are eighty-thousand other people in this town who *do* believe in God! What do you think of those odds, eh?" The grip on my wrist tightened for a second, then he let go. Did I see a fleeting smile?

All through the following day, while a Pacific storm raged, hurling tree branches against the window panes, Nigel's spirit held on to his dwindling body. His flailing arms and tortured face detailed an intense inner struggle. Toward evening, he struggled less. By ten o'clock, he was still. The storm had abated when I left to go home.

Marietta watched her husband's throe's dispassionately, seldom making comment; never showing emotion.

A few hours later, a strong gust of wind rattled my window blinds, and Charlie, my Springer, barked sharply. I knew instantly that Nigel had left us. It was 3.02 Pacific Standard Time. Ten minutes later, Patricia called to confirm it. "He died about three o'clock," she told me in a flat voice.

"I know," I had to say, "he told me. I'll be over shortly."

While I straightened him out and shaved off a week's stubble, I wondered how and when his tattered spirit would come together. My own belief is that parts of our spirit are attached to significant places and people in our lives, and when our physical bodies die, the energy, the spirit, comes together before moving on to its final place in the universe. I guessed that remnants of Nigel's spirit might be in India and with his ex-wife.

The once-tortured face lined with years of pain and bitterness, now lay quiet, alabaster-like and peaceful. Had I joined his hands together as if in prayer, he would have fitted nicely in a corner of Westminster Abbey. From the serenity etched on his face, I guessed that he had found a pilot to take him across the bar.

For the sake of propriety, Marietta attended the memorial service and asked me to take care of his cremated remains. A week later she left the state, married a mountain man – and joined the Hell's Angels.

On a sparkling day in May, I took Nigel's remains into the Northern Sierra Mountains and buried them at the base of an ancient cedar, far from corruption, far from the madding crowd, and certainly a little closer to his Creator.

I find myself obliged to add a short postscript to one of the more poignant episodes of my life, an afterthought that profiles human pathos.

Several weeks after I had scattered Nigel's ashes in the mountains, Marietta called me to tell me that she and her man would be in town on a certain evening, and asked would I join them for dinner at a local restaurant.

While her man was truly a "mountain man,"-- coarse, unkempt and vulgar,-- Marietta had maintained her distinctive looks and style but had exchanged her woolen suit for one of leather trimmed with silver buckles and buttons. I thought she looked more attractive. She managed his dialogue with skill. He ignored me. I sat miserably through the evening wishing I could exchange places with him for just that night.

She sat exquisitely astride the pillion of a Harley Davidson as they drove off, turned and waved to me, smiling.

In little under a year both were dead – killed in a motorcycle accident. I trust she enjoyed her brief freedom.

Once again I began to wonder about God's influence on our lives but this time with skepticism.

# The Curiosity Shop
## Living one day ay a Time

Located on a well known but rather seedy street of this moderately sized northern town, the *Thrift Shop* lay mid-block amid some apartments rented out to those who relied on the government for their monthly stipend, a small dingy bar painted pea green which sold beer garishly advertised by a flickering red neon sign, and a large red brick building trimmed with a white stone parapet, originally owned by a defunct telephone company, but now vacant.

By comparison with its neighbors, including a dilapidated 1920s abandoned movie theatre across the street, the thrift shop was relatively well maintained. Its front window, for instance, had no adhesive tape holding the pane together, the door jamb had not been jimmied and there were no blood stains on the adjacent sidewalk.

Since the store hours were from 10.a.m. until 4.p.m. I was surprised to find ten or twelve people waiting outside when I arrived fifteen minutes before opening time. Three of them were my volunteers; the rest were *"early birds"* eager to snap up any new items which might appear in the window.

The volunteers, a little beyond retirement age, were delightful, two women and a man. They told me that they had worked at the thrift store for several years and knew the quirks about running it from A to Z. They also knew the street people with whom we dealt every day. "Just keep an eye on them and let them know that that's what you are doing, and you'll be fine," was their best advice, and "Don't fall for sob stories or old soldiers tales," was another pearl of advice.

At the rear of the shop, a section was curtained off for privacy: it was where we accepted donations, cleaned them up and priced them. One of the perks of being a volunteer was getting first choice of the donations before they were set out for sale to the public.

Several weeks went by without incident. The weather was still cool and those without homes stayed off the street. When the shop became more crowded, however, I spent most of my shop hours strolling behind the clothes racks and in and out of the dressing closets. Some of the characters became familiar after a while and would disappear behind the taller racks of ladies dresses for rather longer than I deemed reasonable. They were often in the dressing closets trying clothes on, and sometimes stretched out asleep. I found it nearly impossible, without being intrusive, to wait for them to come out to see if they had more clothes on than when they went in I never actually caught one such shoplifter and wondered how I would have handled the situation. "Hey you, take those clothes off." Never do, I concluded after a brief vision of myself being hauled off to jail protesting volubly that I was only trying to stop a burglary-in-progress. I reluctantly decided that an old dress,' bra or two simply weren't worth it, and turned a blind eye on the *closeteers*.

I still continued to patrol that small area, however, just in case I spied someone with obviously ill-concealed contraband. One morning I emerged from between the racks of men's pants and woolen jerseys to find two policemen talking to one of my regular suspects, a nondescript middle-aged woman dressed in an array of gaudy gypsy-like clothes. They all glared at me, "Yeah, that's 'im," she said, "E's been following me about all mornin'."

Both policemen came over toward me. "Good morning, sir. This lady has accused you of following her about all over the place. If that is true, perhaps you might explain to us why?"

The mental image I had had of being connected to the possible goings on in the dressing closets had not come to pass, but this was as close as I might have dared imagine. Trying to keep the irritation out of my voice, I replied, "This lady is wrong. I haven't been following her or anyone else around. I am the manager of this thrift shop and part of my job is to prevent theft. I therefore occasionally walk the store for that very purpose."

The policemen briefly noted what I had said and turned to the woman. "What's 'e say? Did 'e call me a thief?" She appeared to be of Irish extraction for she took up a boxing stance.

One of the cops spoke quietly and apparently convincingly to her for a few minutes. Turning to me, he said, "She's one of our regulars, a little schizophrenic but otherwise harmless. If I may have your name and the telephone number of your employers, sir, we'll be on our way."

By the middle of summer, there had been several more incidents such as that but nobody had accused me of stalking. My trusty volunteers became my true friends. We spent hours chatting over cups of tea. I learned a lot about people, and a lot about myself. Perhaps the greatest lesson I learned was not to take life too seriously and I found myself emulating my newly found friends' gentle ways. I became a kinder man.

The pub next door often proved to be an aggravation. Whether they were thrown out or just staggered out, the inebriate would occasionally somehow find his or her way into the shop. Surrounded by priceless *objéts d'art,* in an unrecognizable world , the unfortunate would first try to find out where he was by yelling at the top of his lungs, "Where the hell am I?" followed shortly by "Lemme get outta here", as he fought his way through pants and dresses on wire coat hangers, pulling them onto the floor in an effort to find the exit. Fortunately this didn't very often happen.

The worst street incident occurred one Friday afternoon just as we were closing. The door of the pub swung violently open and two individuals, the one chasing the other, rocketed out onto the street. This was not a too unusual daily event, but the scream that followed certainly made the hair on the back of my neck bristle. Our hero, knife in hand, knelt beside his victim yelling at him in Spanish. All of my customers took the opportunity to take a ringside seat at the front window, perhaps thanking their lucky stars that they were not involved. The police arrived, seemingly within seconds, and apprehended the stabber, and again with remarkable speed, put the injured man into an ambulance.

The investigating officers invaded the shop and asked if anyone had witnessed the assault. Incredibly, nearly all the men in the shop had seen the "whole thing." Each police officer was given a completely difference aspect of the scene.

"Jumped on 'is back and stabbed 'im in the neck."

"Run up behind 'im and stuck 'im in the back."

"Knocked 'im down, kicked 'im and stabbed 'im in the chest."

Astonished by these individual's individual egotism, I wondered how they could go to such lengths as to invent a scenario for the police for effect only, and not have enough ego to improve the quality of their own lives or those close to them.

There was plenty of life to observe from behind the counter of that shop and to spend several hours each day philosophizing on one's fellow human, but the most important insights into the charitable side of my fellow being, I tried to imitate. Never having been much of a philosopher, I attempted to avoid making harsh, snap judgments and to take into consideration the other person's point of view or circumstance; or to curb my almost natural impatience and sergeant-major-like need for respect, accuracy and formality.

One beautiful June afternoon, when the pub next door was relatively quiet, the usually sparse traffic on Market Street had dwindled to a dribble, and the westering sun pleasantly warmed the body instead of frying it, I let the volunteers go home early, locked the street door and set about counting the intake. Half way through, I thought I heard a noise toward the back. Stopping momentarily to listen more carefully, I reminded myself that I had not walked through the store before satisfying myself that it was empty. Oh well, probably a rat or something. I went on counting. There it was again! A rustle of clothes and the clink of coat hangers; a scene from "The Pawnbroker" flashed through my mind and I had short spasm of panic. Those bloody dressing closets! I knew they would be trouble.

"Excuse me!" I nearly jumped out of my skin. Standing there at the end of a rack of clothes stood a frail elderly lady dressed in a cotton dress and a bolero with pink rosebuds on it. My first thought was "I wonder if that's hers or ours." The she began to shamble toward me. She had a limp and carried one of those three pronged-walking sticks. "Are you closed already?"

"Yes we are, madam." I replied, hoping she could make it to the front door, toward which I was already moving.

"Can't get around like I used to," she said flatly, "I usually get the 3:45 bus back to Anderson, but I think I've left it a bit late, haven't I?" It was now five minutes to four.

"Let me see if it's still there," I said and unlocked the door. There was no sign of the Anderson bus. "'Fraid not," I said and came over to hear what her next suggestion might be.

"O-o-o-o-h, that feels good," she said as she flopped down onto one of my sofas, the $90 one wheezing something awful "Do you think you could call me a senior taxi, sir? They used to run the latecomers down to Anderson in the old days."

"Blimey," I thought, never heard of those. "I'll try the taxi company to see if they have any gratis rides going that way." They didn't and let me know that I must be daft if I thought that any taxi company would give fares a free ride. Playing for time, I said to the dear old soul, whose name was, very appropriately Maggie Wiggins. "Look dear, if I put a chair outside the shop window, on the pavement, you can wait there in the sun and see if you can flag a cab down. You never know, perhaps one'll take you."

A sense of foreboding had enveloped me. It was the sort of feeling you get when you're on a long drive and the oil light has come on twice and gone off – by itself. My Higher Power was doing one of His things again. I wish He wouldn't. I find it upsetting; it exposes my character defects.

Time for me to take the day's cash intake up to the main office, something I did as regularly as clockwork, but what about Maggie? Simply to abandon her on Market Street would be – well, unthinkable.

"Maggie, dear, what do you think you might do if you can't get a taxi?" I asked her, knowing rather well what the outcome of any question would be.

The poor soul was completely nonplussed. Her usual routine had sustained a mortal blow and she simply had no way of readjusting.

"Look, Maggie," I said, "I'll drive you home. It's only about half-an-hour and I have nothing else to do tonight. How's that?"

Her face lit up, and that was enough for me. An enormous obstacle blocking the end of her day had been removed. I felt saintly.

I had just purchased a red MGB. GT, late 1990's vintage. It was the joy of my life. Apart from taking me to and from work, it took me where my memory and my imagination wanted to go; back to Marin County and those days when I was still bonkers. When she saw what I was driving, Maggie let out a very young *"WHOOHIE!"*

Emulating someone she'd seen on some TV ad, she tried to hike her good leg over the door to get into the passenger seat, and got her knickers all twisted up, facing the wrong way.

"You'll do yourself an injury doing that Maggie," I said trying had not to embarrass her more than she already was. "Here, let me open the door – and please buckle up."

Off we went heading for I-5 – and Anderson nine or ten miles south. I knew where this small township was but I certainly didn't know my way around: once off I-5, I was lost.

Strangely enough, Maggie looked quite at home sitting in the bucket seat next to me. Her thinning grey hair streamed out behind her with a small piece of blue ribbon still attached, and her small seventy-odd-year old face seemed to have lost many of its wrinkles of weather, stress and time. She was beaming.

"Did you ever ride in a drop-head coupe before, Maggie?" I yelled at her over the roar of the engine.

She shook her head. "My husband was a crop duster; he took me up once. Except for the smell, this is just like those days. He flew in WWII as a navigator." She explained.

The experience took me back, too, to crazier days when I had spent most of my working hours in harms way as a Marine Investigator – damaged ships, damaged cargo and often damaged people.

"What exit do I take, Maggie?"

"I don't know. The same one as the bus, I suppose."

"I've never taken the bus to Anderson." I began to feel irritated, and decided to take North Street, which seemed to be the main route into Anderson.

"Does this look familiar, Maggie?" I asked, trying not to sound upset.

"The bus drops me off right outside my apartment," said in a smug sort of manner.

Half afraid to ask, I said, "Do you happen to know exactly where you live – I mean the street address?"

"Not really. There's a park nearby and a big tree right on the corner of the street." We had arrived at a big park surrounded by several large trees. I stopped the car under a big tree.

"What about a grocery store?" I asked. "Any close by?"

"Oh, yes. There's a Raley's – or maybe an Albertsons. I forget. I remember the produce is better at one of them."

For all I knew I might well have been in the middle of the Great Wall of China. "I am presuming that this town is Anderson, Maggie. Have you any reason to doubt it?"

Maggie half turned her back on me, drew her jacket about her shoulders, and started to sulk. "Now you've gone all uppity on me. Are you angry at me?"

I thought about the whole adventure for a minute or two, and in particular about a few of the revelations that had come to me during the past six months, and of the resolutions I had made.

"Not really Maggie, just confused. I want to get you home safely, and I want to go home myself, so let's put our heads together and figure out which way to go. Okay?"

"That's alright, Peter, I guess I'm just getting old." I put my arm around her thin shoulders and gave her a squeeze. She relaxed, and when she looked at me again her face bore that radiant smile again. *Got to grow up, Peter* I scolded myself.

Maggie suddenly shouted and began to wave her arms over her head.

"What's up?" I said, hoping her memory had come back. But it was better than that.

"It's Annie – Annie Fox. She lives in the same building as me. *HEY, ANNIE!*"

Could it be the same Anne Fox who was my favorite volunteer? There she was hurrying down the street, arms full of groceries.

"Hi Peter," said Anne with a sparkle in her eye, "Trying to steal a quiet weekend with my friend Maggie?" and winked. "And Maggie, you old tart, I hope you were going to tell me about this romance. What's going on?"

I felt myself blushing as I tried to explain in as few words as I could. Anne cut me short. "You don't have to explain to me, Peter, I understand; thousands wouldn't, but I do." She gave me another dimpled grin.

I drove them down the main street to their apartment block with Anne squeezed into the space behind the driver and passenger seats – big enough for a large suitcase.

Their arrival, especially Anne's exit from the luggage compartment, caused screams of delight from some of their friends gathered outside on the patio enjoying an evening drink.

"Oh my, Annie, who've you picked up tonight – or does he belong to Maggie?

"His name is Peter, and he's my boss," Anne said with mock grandiosity."

"Maggie missed the last bus and Peter kindly drove her home."

Nothing else would do but that I join them around the table and have a cool drink of lemonade before going home.

Like a bouquet of spring flowers, my newfound friends showed off their graces and simple charms.

Dusk was settling over Anderson when I left to drive home. Under ideal driving conditions, a warm breeze pulling at my face and the engine purring like a contented cat, I thought of the seven elderly ladies with whom I had just spent the last hour chatting and joshing. I felt as though I had just had a lesson on life itself; as though I had been sitting at the feet of Gamaliel, for through all their simplicity, I had recognized a great fount of wisdom. I wondered how they managed to be so apparently at peace with the world and concluded that they must have a twelve step program of their own and were simply *living one day at a time.*

# The Dark Side of Cancer Treatment

## A Story of Detached Professionalism

*It is hard to say now when the gut fear began. It was probably when my wife fell while getting out of bed and couldn't get up. With pounding heart and the sick feeling of dread in my stomach, I helped her up and noticed that she was unable to stand on her own. I could see that her condition had deteriorated overnight. We already knew about the effects of radiation and chemo: the burns, the diarrhea and the general exhaustion, but what I saw that morning sowed the seeds of panic.*

*

Gloria, my wife of twenty-two years, is a psychotherapist and a pillar of strength in the local mental health community. Alert and full of life, she embodied all the essences of health.

During the early part of 2005, she occasionally complained of acid reflux and once or twice about minor rectal bleeding. In March she had a colonoscopy to determine the extent of suspected hemorrhoids. The examination revealed a 12mm (L) tumor situated at the inner cusp of the anus. Three days later, the laboratory deemed it malignant. Gloria had cancer. The oncologist told us it was probably relatively new – perhaps twelve weeks old.

Still shaking and partially in denial – how could she, of all people, have cancer? – Gloria declined to undergo immediate radiation treatment and chemotherapy. She wanted to explore other avenues of treatment. Before we left the cancer care unit, she asked about surgery. Both the oncologist and the radiation therapist said that it would probably result in a colostomy – *and we really didn't want that, did we?*

There followed an unnatural stillness about the house. She, stoic and involved in her own tempestuous thoughts, and me, supportive but tiptoeing around her, afraid that I might say something upsetting. It was as though we had a satanic guest in our house. On my own for several hours each day, my panic-stricken mind often wandered to the desolate regions of the *What Ifs* and then reversed course to the reality that my wife had a deadly, loathsome disease – and I thought of the movie *The Exorcism.* I became overwhelmed with fear.

During a moment of clarity, Gloria decided to seek medical treatment without further ado. The treatments were mathematically and clinically laid out for us: fifteen doses of radiation interspersed by five days of intravenously induced 5FU chemical, followed by another fifteen shots of radiation and another five days of chemotherapy. The cancer doctors warned Gloria that the radiation would produce a nasty sunburn-like result, and that the chemo would cause diarrhea, vomiting and general debility.

The medical staff in general was cheerful. I got the impression that they regarded cancer in the same familiar manner as the cardiac unit viewed coronary artery disease – serious but nothing to worry about. Both Gloria and I were, to some degree, comforted.

Gloria continued to work at her job and paid daily visits to the radiation lab; a fifteen minute shot, and that was that. Two weeks later she was admitted to the oncology ward for the chemo intravenous drip. Twenty-four hours a day and daily visits to the radiation lab. By week's end she looked ill: eyes sunken, gray skin and acute diarrhea.

She was discharged a day later than originally scheduled but the radiation was to continue on the following Monday. Barely able to walk, she managed to follow the doctor's instructions.

"Give her a day or two off," I pleaded. They urged that she do her best to continue uninterrupted for, they explained, any break in the routine might cause the radiation treatment to be ineffective.

Two days later, in the early morning, she fell between the bed and the nightstand and couldn't get up; she was simply too weak. I am an old sea captain and used to emergencies, but my wife's plight and her obvious great distress, took me to the gates of panic – and the hospital.

Unable to stand and barely aware of her surroundings, Gloria and I waited to see the radiation therapist. I didn't know him – he was young and apparently new to the hospital cancer team. After five minutes of performing an examination of the region targeted for radiation, I asked him if he had noticed Gloria's condition. He barely acknowledged my presence and continued his examination.

"This woman is very ill," I almost yelled, "she needs immediate medical attention, not radiation." He looked at me dispassionately, and muttered something like "this is normal," and continued with his examination. He reiterated his profound conclusion "Yes, yes, this is normal after chemo and radiation." In my mind I knew that my wife was dying. I again told the doctor that I thought she needed proper medical attention

At that moment, the social worker on the unit came in to see what was happening. One look at Gloria and she rushed off, found another doctor who, after a brief examination, agreed that my wife, indeed showed signs of debility far beyond that normally experienced at this stage of treatment. In half an hour she was in a ward on the cancer unit. Neither her original oncologist nor the radiation therapist attended. At three in the afternoon, Gloria began to cough up mucous. Once again I told the attending doctor that Gloria she needed immediate intensive care. SOMEONE HEARD MY PRAYER! In less time that it took me to plead her case, she was in intensive care – on life support. I had nearly lost my wife.

For five days Gloria teetered on the bank of the River Styx. Toxic shock set in; pneumonia developed as a result of aspirating food into her lungs; the chemo had all but destroyed her immune system and the antibiotics employed to save her life had laid raw her digestive tract. I watched he delicate face, once alive and full of humor, fade and become a pallid mask. Each time I entered her cubicle, my heart beating rapidly, I glanced first at her breast to see if it was moving, and then at her face festooned with plastic tubes all beneath an oxygen mask. I heard her talking hysterical nonsense into her mask and watched her gag as the contents of her stomach were sucked out.

My hyperactive mind wanted to know the answers to many questions, but first I had to come to grips with the utter grief, the anger and bewilderment. From a seemingly diminutive wart-like growth at the lower end of the colon, which may well have been excised during its early stage, my wife had been reduced to an inert frame. Was it the cure that had almost killed her? Had the doctors overdosed her with 5FU? Why had the oncology doctors not come to see her? Did they care? Did they know? Did they want to know? The doctor in charge of the ICU, however, knew his craft; he was a man who cared. After ten days in Intensive Care, Gloria was considered well enough to be moved down to the oncology ward to begin the long, excruciating return to normalcy.

Day after day she experienced uncontrollable diarrhea and vomiting that cost her forty pounds in body weight and most of her hair – a daily reminder that 5FU chemo was still in her system.

Gloria's discipline and her determination to live gradually gained the upper hand. With care and humor, the nurses on the floor saw her through this near-catastrophe and were there to cheer her on the day she left for home.

The aftermath of this terrible experience was the legacy of 5FU. Gloria's digestive system, raw and unprotected from its killing effects, is still healing. Her finger and toenails decayed and fell off. But I think that far worse than any of the physical wreckage left by this disease is the psychological fear of its return.

A subsequent examination of the site tumor site showed that it had been wiped out – nothing remained. The ironical parting words of the attending radiation therapist, "Well, we've cured you."

For my own part, as a deeply involved significant other, I am thankful that there remains a nucleus of good medical professionals. There is, however, a certain rigidity among the medical practitioners who administer radiation and advise on the treatment of cancer. Their adherence to protocol appears to diminish their capacity for compassion. In their eagerness to cure, they must remember that we are not bionic creatures; we have limitations, especially when poisonous chemicals are introduced into the system without prior testing to ascertain if this particular patient can take it.

There are two further legacies that evolve from having triumphed over this disease: The joy of having reached a safe harbor, and a bill for $241,000.00! The first of which we earnestly pray will last for the rest of our lives, the second probably will!

Nine months have elapsed since Gloria was declared cancer-free. She and I have discussed the grim days and the sunny days: it is time to reflect on the effects it has had on our lives – and to share some advice,

We advise all patients who visit a doctor not to be afraid of him. Ask questions, even dumb questions. Don't let them bully you. If you are not clear about anything, make sure you understand before you leave the doctor's office. Take notes.

Make sure that the doctors exhaust all options for treatment before you agree to whatever they have recommended.

If you have cancer, make sure they do all the necessary blood tests before beginning chemo. A low white blood cell count is essential to determine that the chemical will not kill you.

Don't be a "good" patient – it may not be good for your health.

*

*Redding, California*
*March 6, 2005.*

Gloria Aeilts-Wright, my beloved wife of twenty-four years, took on her Pilot during the early hours of Monday morning August 24, 2009 and entered her last port-of-call at 02.15. She was a mere sixty-three years of age; a victim of cancer.